THE DEPTH OF DARKNESS

by

Kevin Craig Mortimer

Part 1

Map of Outer Systems, 3050–07

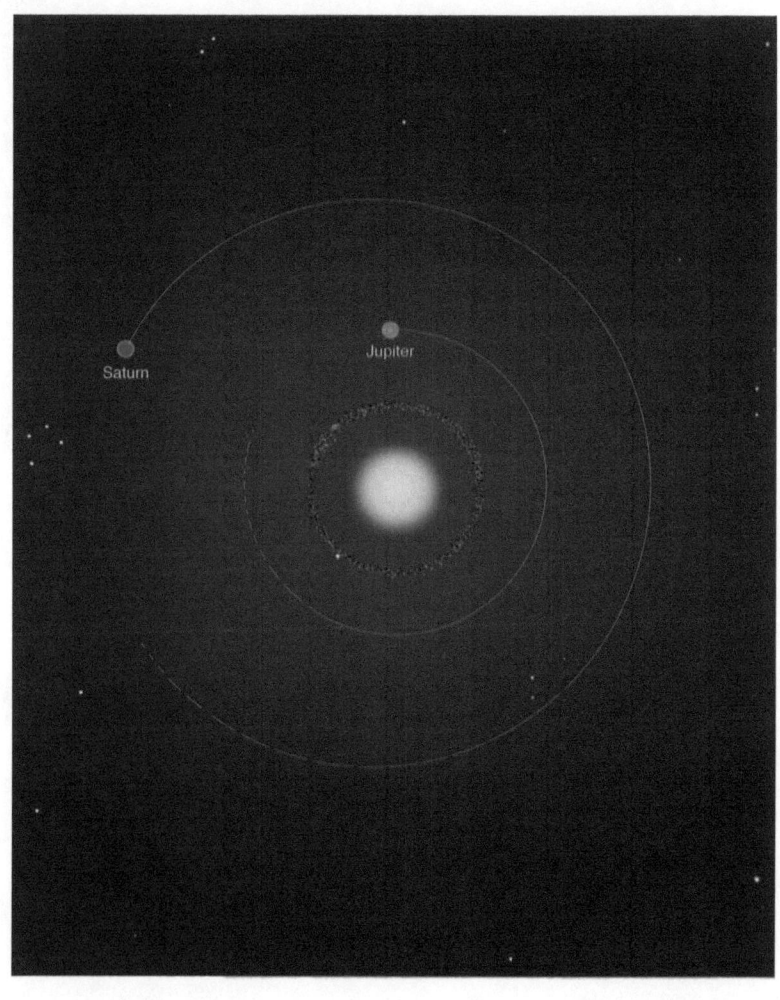

CHAPTER ONE

The sun was just rising and, with it, River Goldstein felt the usual sense of happiness the moment brought. It was a fortunate turn of events that had allowed him to suddenly find himself shortlisted to complete his PhD at the most famous of research facilities. The cresting sun was a bright spot of white light creeping beyond the black orb of the planet. The icy crystals and dust particles of Saturn's rings highlighted the glorious light as it beamed towards the facility, banishing the depth of the vacuum's darkness.

His attention wandered to the approaching vessel, its graceful sweeps a shadow against the backdrop of the sun, making the exact features of the ship unrecognisable. In the vastness of space the lack of real gravity made landing a spacecraft easier, but it still had its challenges. The approaching vessel kept firing off small bursts of carbon dioxide from the oxygen scrubbers in a multitude of directions, either individually or together, to slow the ship down or to turn it so that the belly of the hull was in even alignment with the opening that led down to the landing deck.

It was still beyond the range of the artificial gravity of the platform and was steadily gliding towards its designated berthing. A thrust of gas took it out of sight and River turned from the window that looked out at Saturn and went to stand in anticipation at a different window that looked onto the hexagonal landing deck. The arriving ship brought a shipment of highly classified matter. The whole facility was practically buzzing with excitement at what such a prospect entailed. The landing deck was bathed in flickering red glow from the warning lights that signalled an open airlock. As the ship neared, the details were revealed in red hues. Two bright spotlights flared to life as the pilot switched on his visual assistance, obviously deciding that the radar was no longer sufficient.

Ironic that in this day and age, man still finds comfort in using his own senses, mused River.

Hatches slid aside followed by the landing gear unfurling from the hull, like the legs of a giant insect. The ship looked like a large dragonfly, the designer of the craft having taken inspiration from Earth's natural beauty. Mechanics dressed in spacesuits came walking out from the inner airlock, their steps made ungainly by the imitation gravity. The ship landed heavily, the landing gears compacting noticeably as they absorbed the impact.

The mechanics walked around the settled ship and began fitting an assortment of hoses and other cabling to it at various points as the outer airlock slowly began to close. Steam filled the landing area as soon as the outer doors had closed. The passengers and its cargo would soon be offloaded. River, having seen enough, decided it was time to head down to the airlock and greet the new arrivals.

It was an exciting moment for River. It was not very often that visitors made it all the way out to the facility. Only the fastest ships could make it out to Saturn in anything less than three months of flight; a ninety day voyage at least did not require stasis. Anything quicker would need hibernation in a stasis chamber to withstand the forces that could crush a body into its molecular building blocks. The Human Earth Confederacy, or HEC, only had a handful of these craft with more being built in the construction facilities on Luna. The dragonfly-inspired ship in the berthing was one of these, and there were only two of them in the fleet as far as River knew. Only the best pilots were allowed anywhere near these ships. Of course, should River's research finish successfully, then a whole new manner of travel would be available and distances would not be as insurmountable as they were now.

Rather than use the main elevator, River chose to scamper down a small maintenance ladder; the inner airlock was only one floor below and easily accessible. A short climb brought him into a corridor full of activity as a number of travel-weary arrivals met eager tenants. With the outer airlock closed, the inner airlock was opened fully so that offloading could be handled efficiently. River had to push his way through the throng of people to get into the landing berth. Once inside, he stepped to the side to get out the way of those that had work to do. The pressure was still equalising inside the massive chamber, as oxygen was being pumped in and heated to establish the same temperature as the rest of the station. Outside in the darkness of space the temperature could be as low as minus two hundred degrees. River, like all other humans, preferred temperature ranges in the low twenties.

The ramp descended from the aft of the ship and River watched to see what was being extricated. A whole team of bodies was milling at the top of the ramp, busy in an organised chaos negotiating a large metal container on wheels. The lead scientist of the facility was standing below, shouting instructions at everyone. Tiernan Edison-McAuley was a beast of a man, not in physique but in character. Boorish and rude, he had the ability to instantly alienate any individual that was not party to accepting his nature. In this solar system there were frightfully few people who had to accept his character, but his abrasiveness was tolerated by those that mattered, and so he got away with it. He was, however, unquestionably intelligent and had held the position of lead scientist at the research facility in the orbit of Titan for almost twenty years. Countless discoveries could be attributed to his brilliance, which had fuelled his megalomania and arrogance. River and Professor Edison did not get along well.

Eventually the team succeeded in aligning the crate with the exit and slowly the massive steel rectangle began to roll down the ramp towards the facility itself. A smirking Edison followed the procession. He passed River without so much as a glance. The young man put his irritating superior out of his mind and looked up at the metal dragonfly.

Three figures remained at the head of the ramp and were conferring with each other. One was undoubtedly the person River had been waiting for. The others turned and headed back into the ship, which started down the ramp. River approached the foot, and as the figure withdrew his helmet River shouted out in welcome.

"About time you managed to bring yourself out here to the Saucer!"

"River, you bookworm. Glad to see you're still alive," joked his long-unseen friend. They had grown up together and the years had not diminished the confidence of the man. In looks he had followed his father to the letter; he had the exact same pose and loud booming voice.

"Although I might slowly be dying of boredom out here."

"Come on, it can't be all that bad. Isn't this what you've always wanted?"

"Yeah, I guess it is. But you probably want to get refreshed. Come, let me walk with you to your dorm and then we can meet in the rec-area?"

"That sounds really good, six weeks of stasis is a little too much for me."

"Six weeks? You obviously have not been out to Gliese! That's a good fourteen years," laughed River, slapping Stuart on the back as he guided him into the facility.

#

River had shown Stuart to his rooms and then made his way to the recreation area to wait for his friend while he refreshed himself and took care of any unmentionables that might have accumulated during stasis. The discovery of stasis was incredible but it did have its drawbacks; heavy constipation was one of the very unfortunate ones.

An ensemble of characters used the recreation area. Paraphernalia that represented the history and culture of the many different creeds of human life that populated the research facility decorated shelves and the walls. While all the scientists were at most times a sombre crowd of individuals, they did have the odd occasion where they would relax and let their austere guards down and celebrate like recently graduated students. From the walls hung flags from various territories and nations, accompanied by other props like antler racks and number plates. The rec-area was just like a mid-western pub out on some bizarre desert route. Although, in this case, the desert route was a frigid dark void with no oxygen, millions of kilometres away from the nearest self-sustaining civilisation.

The sliding doors shut with a subtle clank behind River as he stepped down into the large room. A large, single window that showed the Saturnian moon of Titan with its yellow methane atmosphere dominated the far wall. Walking into the rec-area always made River feel like he was stepping out into the darkness of space. The visage of the outside created the sensation of being drawn out into the nothingness. He knew it was his general susceptibility to anxiety and always had to work to bring it under control. A few minutes sitting at a table would calm him and he would grow more comfortable until eventually he would forget about it.

He ordered himself a light Martian beer, a reddish pilsner brew that contained practically no alcohol; he still intended heading back to the laboratory later in the evening to complete some paperwork on the results of his experiments earlier in the day. He paid by swiping his access card rather than using cash. Cold, hard cash was rare on any of the remote facilities, regardless of their nature. Credits were the more common form of payment.

When he was halfway through his beer the doors to the rec-area slid open to allow Stuart in. As most people seemed to be, Stuart was taken in by the sight of Titan through the large window, but unlike River he recovered quickly and scanned through the room finding his friend. He casually strolled up and pulled back a chair, flipped it around to bring the backrest to the front and straddled the chair, leaning with his chest against it.

"Feels good to be clean and refreshed. I don't think I'll ever get used to stasis, but the discomfort is worth it for the flying," he declared with a glint of amusement in his eyes. "So what are you guys working on so far away from home?"

"You know I can't talk to you about that," chuckled River.

"Yeah, I guess not. RF601 is very secretive."

"And with good reason, most of what we work with here is still too experimental and potentially dangerous for the knowledge and details to become public domain."

"Yeah, yeah, spare me the lecture," sighed Stuart.

"So how have you been in general? You planning on hanging around here much longer?"

"I've been well, actually. No place is perfect, but it's an immense honour to be working here with the distinguished people that make this their home and office."

"Distinguished?" asked Stuart incredulously.

"Well, yes." River was confused. The saucer of RF601 was the leading research facility in the solar system, and all of the greatest advancements of the last three decades had been discovered in the top-secret laboratories.

"I'm just winding you up. I'm happy for you. Tell you what, let me order you a congratulatory shot of something."

"No, Stuey. I still need to work."

"Come on, Riv, how often do I get to sit and have a drink with you?" pleaded Stuart. "Besides, I ship out in two days' time. After we've refuelled and restocked I'm off to meet up with the Jovian Sector Border Patrols."

"Is Jupiter all the way on the other side of the sun? I don't quite realise the planetary orbits."

"Well, why should you? It's part of my job, not yours," grinned Stuart. "No, Jupiter isn't on the other side, it's in line, so still a long way away. So? How 'bout it?"

"Oh, all right then."

With a hoot of victory Stuart jumped up and headed over to the bar counter to elicit the shots and a drink for himself. He returned promptly after having been served quickly and efficiently. The rec-area was quiet, but would be filling up soon. Stuart placed the two shots of clear liquor down on the table and placed his bottle of the same Martian beer, only the normal lager variety, next to the two shots.

"What did you get?"

"Dunno, I just asked for the strongest shot they have." He was still grinning. It was the winning grin that he had always displayed whenever he'd managed to convince his studious friend to defy the normalities of his sober world.

"To your successes," toasted Stuart.

"I wouldn't tip that back," came a dry and hoarse voice from the closing doors of the rec-area. Edison had chosen to arrive on the scene, much to River's disappointment. The old man seemed to materialise out of thin air frequently. River suspected it was purely to upset his plans.

"Sir, I'm on break?"

Stuart looked perplexed, but bit his tongue; being a military man he understood the dynamic between superior and inferior. Instead he watched the exchange intently.

"I'm calling all non-active personnel back on duty. The newly arrived samples are taking the utmost priority now, and I won't have you drunk at your post," stated the old scientist coldly.

"Why?" asked River suspiciously.

"I will not be questioned by someone such as yourself. Get yourself decontaminated immediately. We begin working on the samples tonight," concluded Edison. He marched off without waiting for a reply.

River sighed loudly. "I guess I'm left with no choice. We'll have to catch up another time."

"No use letting good liquor go to waste," declared Stuart, dropping his shot and tucking away River's with equal zeal. He pulled his face at the strength of the liquor. "Wow! That stuff is like paint stripper. Love it."

CHAPTER TWO

River walked into the laboratory where a crew of technicians were busy pulling a smaller container out of the shipping crate that had been brought in on Stuart's ship. The container slid out on rails and once it was clear of the shipping crate, the technicians unfolded castor wheels from underneath it, detached it from the rails and wheeled it clear.

Edison was watching them perform their task without emotion, occasionally wiping at his nose with his handkerchief. It was his normal nervous trait, one that most people seldom noticed these days. River found it extraordinarily strange that in an environment such as the Saucer's, Edison should always be ill with a cold.

Perhaps he's just allergic to something in the climate control? he wondered idly.

Three of the technicians removed the shipping crate while the remaining one began to remove the protective padding from the smaller container. With the padding gone, River recognised the container to be a cryogenic stasis chamber, a smaller one for non-human biological matter. He glanced up at Edison as the last technician left.

Once the doors to the laboratory had closed and only authorised personnel were in attendance, Edison spoke. "Yes, Professor Goldstein, you have some biological matter to examine, alien in its supposed origin."

"Alien." River played out the word slowly, almost as if he had heard it for the first time.

He quickly rushed up the three steps to the cryo-chamber and knelt next to the controls. It was set to a temperature of minus one hundred degrees Celsius. At that temperature nothing could survive; or at least, to the knowledge of current scientific reasoning. He quickly checked the battery levels. They were at fifteen per cent.

"Sir, the batteries are running low. May I move the cryo-chamber into the main laboratory immediately, so that it can be connected to facility power?" he requested.

Edison nodded his assent, although strictly speaking this was River's speciality and Edison would've been amiss to countermand his request.

River pushed the cryo-chamber towards the decontamination sluice that would, using ultraviolet radiation, destroy any micro-bacteria that might have settled on the outer shell. This was necessary before it was allowed into the inner section of the laboratory. River would have to enter the inner section through another entrance after having changed into overalls before stepping into a similar, though less hazardous, decontamination sluice. The process did not take long to complete and soon enough River had connected the cryo-chamber to a fixed power source. The other scientists had changed into their laboratory overalls while he had worked with the chamber and were now in the process of entering the inner section themselves.

Edison was the last to arrive and after taking his place at the head of the examination table he began directing a variety of commands to all those in attendance. "Professor Goldstein, if you would please remove the sample from the cryo-chamber and place it on the examination table."

River knelt next to the cryo-chamber. It was no longer than a metre and only roughly fifty centimetres wide. The actual chamber in which matter could be stored at temperatures below two hundred Kelvin was relatively small in comparison with the rest of the unit, its height being primarily due to all the engineering required to power and facilitate the freezing process. River deftly punched in a sequence of command instructions on the lit cluster of buttons. They were industrially sized and hardened against the rough use of the typical space jocks and cargo handlers. With a loud hiss the three centimetre thick glass slid aside and cold gas billowed out of the opened chamber. Once the gas had cleared, River saw the sample of biological matter for the first time.

"Well, don't just stand there gawking at it," complained Edison from behind him.

River shook his head in an odd attempt at banishing his unprofessional behaviour and reached in to lift out the tiny little sample. It was roughly the size of a fully grown man's little finger, no longer than six centimetres. Similar to how Terran centipedes had hundreds of tiny legs, this sample had similar appendages. Only whereas a centipede had distinct joints that indicated that the appendages were designed to provide propulsion, these looked more like barbs.

River placed the sample on the large examination table, feeling a little silly at the concept of seven scientists standing around such a small sample in a manner that suggested that they would be working on something significantly larger and more tangible. Edison, seemingly able to read River's thought, mockingly announced, "Do not let the size of the sample detract from what it signifies."

"What you see before you is a new, uncategorised life form that provides a very real danger to human interplanetary society. It is our job to understand what exactly this life form is, its strengths and weaknesses, as well as to define what exactly the parameters of this threat can and would be if left unchecked or unresearched. Now, I can only assume that this life form is already causing havoc out there, but the details thereof are strictly classified and I have not been told about those as yet."

"What timeframe do we have?" asked River.

"We don't have a timeframe, HEC HQ wants our results and evaluations as soon as possible. Professor Goldstein, I suggest you and your team get started."

River nodded absentmindedly. He had been expecting the answer and was already off considering his next move. He reached behind his back, blindly feeling for the keyboard of the console, he traced his fingers along the keys and initiated the recording function in the laboratory. Numerous cameras and microphones strategically placed in the room would now record every little detail that occurred in the laboratory. It was impossible for the scientists to recall days later all the information as it had occurred. The recordings would ensure that only one version of the truth existed.

"First, let us confirm whether the subject has the ability to survive cryostasis. That will give us an idea of the hardiness of the life form. If the subject is dead, then we will begin with dissection to determine basic organism composition and in the process we can determine if the life form is carbon-based like ourselves and other earthly creatures," suggested River rhetorically.

One of the scientists, Shiori Wu he thought her name was, moved to retrieve the scanner that would detect the typical signs of life that known organisms needed to show to be determinable as alive. She had recently arrived at the Saucer from Earth. The jury was still out on her abilities as a scientist, though to date she had performed the tasks he had set for her admirably.

She passed the scanner over the tiny frozen life

form. The top of the scanner had a small display that pulsed with a red light as it scanned; the light would turn green if there was a part of an organic substance that contained life. Scanning a larger body could show that one part of a body was beyond saving and others were not. In the case of the small life form before them there was no sweeping of a large surface, merely holding the scanner over the tiny organism. The instrument continued pulsing red.

"Professor, I'm not sure this is a viable test," suggested Shiori.

"How come?" asked Edison, interrupting the process from which he had originally excluded himself.

Shiori looked cornered and unsure of herself. She stammered a reply. "The scanner is designed for use on a much larger organism. It may not be capable of accurately determining this subject's vital statistics."

"Nonsense, this scanner can be used on a bee and it will detect life or no life. If the scanner says it is dead, then it is dead."

River spoke up to take the conversation and focus away from the accuracy of the scanner and, rather, to concentrate on the investigation of the little life form. "Let's begin the thawing process, it won't be necessary to consider the removal of cryostasis only to thaw without damaging any cell structure."

A different scientist, another young arrival, brought a small metal pot with numerous electrical connection points. It was placed over the frozen sample. The pot was a type of microwave cooker, only it used a concentrated beam of low frequency microwaves that did not destroy or cook cells, but only focused on heating up the fibrous tissue in the cells. The agitation of the cells would cause the organism to shake off the cryostasis much more slowly than in a full strength microwave and therefore remain more intact.

The pot hummed steadily as the microwaves were being emitted. Through a small transparent section of the pot, the scientists could observe the subject within. It seemed to be stirring and a whitish light began to pulse in the centre of the little worm-like life form. It began to thrash about. The pot rattled above it and threatened to overturn.

"It isn't dead!" shouted Shiori.

"Quickly, someone pin the microwave emitter down!" roared Edison, who was backing away.

River launched himself at the pot, just as it overturned and the life form seemed to catapult off the examination table. It scurried towards a cluster of stacked equipment and disappeared into a tiny grate that fed air into the laboratory.

"Damn it!" cursed River. "We have found and lost a new life form in the space of ten minutes."

CHAPTER THREE

The loud and incessant hooting noise of River's alarm clock brought him fully back into the world of consciousness. Still drunk with sleep, he slowly pushed the thin comforter blanket aside and with supreme effort managed to swing his body into an upright position. He killed the alarm with minimal celebration and sighed resignedly. It had been two days since the life form had vanished into the air vent and, with that, disappeared with no trace. Not knowing what this newly discovered life form represented and what danger to man it presented, the scientists had set off with minimal excitement, or energy, to find the little organism and bring it back for further study.

Edison had been furious. He had rampaged and screamed out the levels of incompetence he felt them to possess. Thereafter he had stormed off to find a place of quiet contemplation or whatever it was that Edison did – River hardly had an interest in finding out that detail. Edison's fury had cast a dim atmosphere into the laboratory and River had ordered the search to be started before retreating back to his private sanctuary. He had decided that he would continue working on his pet project and ultimately his reason for being at the Saucer. The HEC saw the possibilities for his experimentation and had simply decided that it would not do to have River working for a private consortium that would be able to horde, patent and sell the technology for billions of credits.

River was in danger of stagnating with his research. A significant amount of time had passed since he had last made any real progress with his work, and he was beginning to think that he might need to step back to the absolute basics. Perhaps even as far back as what the accepted rules of nature were. It could very likely be that he needed to challenge the reality of time and space to make his next breakthrough.

That would require a significant paradigm shift. I think I should contact HEC HQ and see about moving to a new facility. One where I receive better support, he considered. "I think I should send out an exploratory query," he concluded aloud.

It was a strange habit for one who should be pragmatic, but River often found that making a decision statement aloud was a firm way of committing himself to a decision. Society was sceptical of people who did that, though, and so River had learnt to not make those statements in earshot of any other people.

On shaky, sleep-heavy legs he made his way from his bed towards his com-console and fell heavily into the padded chair that had not been pushed in under the desk. His rooms were slightly larger than those of some of the scientists, due to his ranking and time on the Saucer, but they were still cramped. All the plastics in the room were white, with thin blue lines painted in the crevices between larger panels. Still, due to the fact that most panels were large and cast from a single strip of plastic, white was by far the prominent colour in the room. The com-console came out of standby quickly and showed a barrage of received messages. From the first subject line, River could see that he had forgotten his own birthday again, but all his loving friends and families probably had reminders going off this morning and so had begun to send through the expected well wishes. He spent a brief amount of time selecting all the messages, and marking them as read before moving them off into a subfolder.

He tapped the screen to compose a new message and addressed it to the Head of Scientific Research,

Human Earth Confederacy. He spent roughly twenty minutes composing and reviewing his request. He had to make sure that he didn't implicate Edison in any way for a number of reasons. Firstly, the top woman of the science division would undoubtedly contact Edison for comment and River did not want any animosity to spoil his chances. Secondly, she had little patience for people who could not sort out their issues and challenges through direct confrontation. River had only met her three times, twice during the awarding ceremonies for his two doctorates and then the third time when he'd found out that his experiments had caught the eye of the Confederacy and that he would be reassigned for duty, away from RF1501, the research facility on the Moon, and to the Saucer, RF601. That had been almost four years ago. Back then she had struck him as a woman who knew exactly what it was that she wanted and that she expected all working under her to know that and fully buy into what she wanted. She had wanted him here at RF601.

River hovered his index finger above the send button for a very long time, before taking a deep breath and tapping the button as he exhaled. The Outbox icon flashed bold briefly and then the message was gone. It was done, his request was sent and he may be on the precipice of either doom or a bright future in the coming days. It took a number of hours for digital communications to travel the distances of darkness between the planets and then there was still the timeframe for discussion and thought to take into account.

"Nothing for it but to continue on as usual. Let us commence day three of searching for that little life form," he said, discarding his sleeping trunks and stepping into the shower. Water was precious in a space station, but the shower water could easily be recycled and used again. Humankind had spent many years perfecting that art.

#

River entered the meeting room precisely an hour after waking up. He was the only one aside from Edison who was punctual; the remaining staffing was late. He chose not to say anything to his superior, as keeping up false pretences was not something he was very comfortable with and invariably he would struggle to keep a harsh tone out of his voice. Instead he helped himself to some coffee that had been brewing at the counter and seated himself at the far end of the table. Coffee was a rare treat out in space. The beans would not grow in containment and with the long time it took to fly out to the station, coffee was usually only brought along as a gift rather than stocked as part of the supplies. He enjoyed the taste slowly and did not rush to finish his cup. The other staffing began to sidle into the room shortly after he had seated himself and within ten minutes the room was full.

River endured some of the well wishes, most being delivered warmheartedly. Only Edison chose not to wish him anything. River was not surprised.

"Let us get this meeting underway," announced Edison. "Prof. Goldstein, could you please provide me with some feedback on your searching and then also your research?"

It was unsurprising that River had been targeted first, but he had nothing to feel ashamed about and so he steadily answered, "On the search for the missing life form, we have made no progress whatsoever. On my research, I feel I might have hit a brick wall. I need to revert back to basics and take it from there."

Edison fixed him with a penetrating gaze. "What do

you mean brick wall?"

"Well, I can't seem to get objects to accelerate beyond a certain point. Although, according to all theoretical paperwork and calculations, the objects should be able to accelerate well beyond that point."

"What is the acceleration point that you cannot break?"

"It's not a matter of not being able to break the acceleration point, it's the challenge I face when I use substantially massive objects. With smaller particles, I am able to achieve the figures I am hoping to achieve."

"So it comes down to a matter of force, then."

"Yes, I suppose it does."

"I'm sure you will think of something. Dr Carson, could you please provide me with some feedback on your searching?" And with that Edison had moved on to the next scientist in line. River was a little stunned that for the first time in his remembrance Edison had said something slightly encouraging. And his simple line of questioning had brought him back to one of the most basic formulations in science, $F=ma$. His mind instantly began to reconsider many of his calculations.

"Professor Goldstein!"

River snapped back to reality. "Yes, Professor Edison?"

"So nice of you to join us." The sarcasm was back, River noted. "I was saying that it is of the utmost importance that you locate the missing life form. I have a communication from HQ that no more samples are available to us and we must discover the nature of this life form. I will accept no failure here. Have I made myself clear?"

Edison waited until River confirmed his understanding of the instruction before continuing. "OK, ladies and gentlemen, the meeting is dismissed."

The room emptied quickly to the sound of chairs

being scraped back and mumbled conversations. River followed the procession out and made a beeline for the exit of the office section. The disc-shaped space station was divided into quadrants, though all the souls on board merely referred to them as sections - the most important of which was the laboratories quadrant. This was the sole purpose of the facility. The remaining three sections were necessary requirements to sustain life on board the facility. They were administration, residential and engineering. Meetings took place in the administration section, whereas all life support machinery and the various transport berthing areas were to be found in engineering. A long column that extended well beyond the diameter of the station pierced the disc; it housed the gravitational field generator, as well as the shield generator and some defensive cannons that retracted into the structure itself when not needed. The column also stored fuel for any passing ships, as well as solar panels for energy creation. A long curving corridor that ran along the inner circumference connected all four quadrants and the column. It was for this corridor that River was heading with urgency before Edison could find a reason to call him back. The reminder of the most basic formula had sparked off a memory, which River was urgently seeking to explore further.

As he slipped through the door into the main corridor he heard, on the edges of his peripheral consciousness, someone calling out his name but he ignored it. He needed to see his friend off and he was leaving in less than an hour.

CHAPTER FOUR

Stuart was rigged up in his flight suit and standing at the base of the access ramp into his ship, the *Benevolent*. She was his pride and his one-and-only. Most pilots developed an almost unhealthy love and dedication for their ships, and he was no different. He clasped River's arm one last time in farewell, forearm to forearm, the hands gripping just below the crook of the inner elbow. It was the traditional greeting from their homeland back on Earth.

His friend had his usual soppy expression on his face. Stuart had to stifle a laugh. "OK, Riv, I need to be on my way. Good luck."

"Good luck to you, too," echoed his friend.

As Stuart stood looking at his friend he heard a burst of energy from the engines of the *Benevolent* and the whine of the fission reactor deep in the bowels of the hull. He still needed to speak with his friend, but his time was up and he needed to be on his way.

"Riv?"

"Yeah?"

"We need to speak. When I'm done with this trip. I'll come back here." The engines were getting louder, and the overhead buzzer below the ramp began to make the customary warning alarm that the ramp would need to be closed soon.

"What is it?"

"Can't talk now, need to go. See you," he shouted over the noise of the engines. "You need to get into the airlock, the outer doors will be opening soon."

River nodded and ran for the inner airlock doors that were beginning to slowly close. His friend made it in enough time. He quickly rushed up the ramp while it was lifting to seal up with the hull of his ship. Inside the *Benevolent* the volume levels were far more bearable, the loud whining noise audible from the outside instead was just a rhythmic rumble.

While the *Benevolent* was a large ship, she was by no means expansive and luxurious. Ultimately she was designed to reach one end of the solar system quickly and without much fuss. Her job was as a high priority courier and as a deep space exploration vessel. Travelling from Titan to Ganymede could almost be named a typical assignment. Only the trip would not be as simple as that. Jupiter was exactly ninety degrees behind Saturn on its orbit, adjacent to the sun. Stuart was going to have to plot a course that would require avoiding many space objects and the sun itself, not just a straight line. Most of the flight would be on autopilot, with the crew in stasis. And even then the flight would take three months.

Stuart made his way into the cockpit and settled himself at the pilot's chair. His co-pilot was in the engine room seeing to other things. Stuart was needed for the take-off in here; this part he could handle with his eyes closed. He searched the viewing ports for the face of his friend and found it above the airlock doors, a level above. The cockpit was lower than the viewing port, but Stuart was still afforded a good view due to the high visibility of the *Benevolent*'s insect inspired shape.

He was overcome with a strange feeling that he could not place, and he was anxious to understand what it meant or if it was just his own tendency for anxiety.

The airlock overhead opened finally and the remaining air that had not been sucked out by the station's recycling and preservation systems was forcibly sucked out into the vacuum. The gravitational core of RF601 still held on to the *Benevolent* firmly, however. Stuart would have to initiate lift-off himself and that was a good thing; it allowed him to control their exit safely through the airlock, rather than to drift out into space and clip an immovable structure of any sort.

He shook his feelings off and began the take-off sequence.

#

The insect-like ship shuddered as the jets applied their energy to the deck and began to fight the gravitational field of the space station. The airlock had opened and all the breathable air had already disappeared. The deck was cleared of all techs and soon the heat from the jets would make the berthing dangerous to anything living in it.

So bloody simple, thought River. *Force is Mass and Acceleration, I can see it happening right in front of me."*

A wash of energy turned to visible heat flowed over the metal decking, the still-present gravity making the sight familiar. Suddenly the ship lifted up, suspended above the decking for a moment and then began to rise higher and higher. River tore his gaze from the heat energy and searched the cockpit viewports in an attempt to spot his friend piloting the craft. But the transparisteel was tinted the same gunmetal grey as the actual armoured plates and so he couldn't see him. Soon enough the ship had cleared the outer airlock. In a reverse of his steps two days prior, River turned to look out of the other windows to see the ship activate its primary propulsion and blast off. It quickly dwindled into insignificance.

"Travel safely," he said quietly. It was then that it dawned on him.

#

Stuart couldn't help but smile at the sensation of leaving the gravitational pull of the space station and then the feeling of weightlessness taking over. He checked his aft camera and watched the Saucer grow smaller as the distance grew. He eased back on the throttle control; the change in power was unnoticeable. He reached out for the switch that would activate the announcement system.

"I am activating the *Benevolent*'s artificial gravitation systems in five, four, three, two, one." He flipped the switch and felt his body being drawn into the seat as the gravity increased. According to protocol he should have followed his announcement with a second one that stated that the crew could begin their preparations for the long-distance flight, but his crew had been working together for enough time that these tasks were well rehearsed. Where possible he had implemented a buddy system and in most pairings the teams could almost work in synchronicity without words. A valuable trait when communications were down and without molecules to carry sound.

He began the process of plotting his route through the solar system. It was a quick process, with the navigation systems completing most of the calculations necessary to account for the movement of space objects. The trick would be any floating debris that they may encounter. The *Benevolent* was equipped with magnetic deflection fields that would assist with protecting against any smaller debris, but for anything of significant size the automated cannon defences would need to be called into action. Human intervention during the deeper stages of space flight would be too slow in coming. Recovery from stasis was not a quick process and disorientation was normal.

Stuart swung himself from his chair and walked into the common area of the ship. It was the one area where all meetings took place, whether for mess, strategy or combat readiness. Their stasis chambers were just below the common area in the medical bay. The *Benevolent* was mostly a single deck ship; only in the middle was she high enough to allow for a second deck.

"Crew," he began, waiting for the clamour to settle. "This will be a long one, three months in stasis and then we arrive just outside a hotspot. As you all know the HEC GSOL war is in full force, and why Command is sending us in there I don't know yet. I am told the instructions will be released to us when we come out of sub-light speed."

"Another suicide mission?" asked his chief tech, Ed Turner, a man as grizzled and cynical as was ever born into this universe.

"We don't know that yet, Ed," answered his chief med tech, Dav Sensler, his thick grey moustache making it look like he delivered his response with a big smile. In truth Dav was constantly smiling. An oddity considering the gloom he had experienced in his life as a doctor on board a military-classed space vessel.

"Any hints as to what is going to be expected of us?" asked the junior med tech, Kim van den Bout. She was still the innocent type, starry-eyed and young.

"No hints, Kim," chuckled Stuart. "HEC Command isn't in the habit of giving anything away. All there is to it is for us to stay sharp and expect the unexpected. I've set the navi-computer to drop us out of sub-light a week ahead of schedule."

"A week!" exclaimed Ed, interrupting Stuart.

"Yes, a week. In the scheme of things, Ed, a week is nothing. But it will give us plenty of time to get over our stasis disorientation and be alert to any kind of attack. You might be keen on a tough fight, but I'd sooner not take my chances. Don't forget, a three month stasis is far longer than any of us usually has to endure."

Ed nodded in agreement, thinking the details through.

Kim looked up from her fingernail examination, a thought evidently etched across her forehead. "Captain, do you suspect the fighting to be thick around Ganymede? Where are most of the engagements being fought?"

"Hard to tell." Stuart paused, thinking. "I haven't been following the reports too closely, but as I understand it most of the fighting is happening in the asteroid belt. HEC and GSOL are vying for the most profitable mining 'roids."

"So we should be quite far from it all?" she asked again.

"We can't assume zero danger," answered Ed for Stuart. "GSOL will always have patrols so near their home, and Ganymede is almost the same size as Mother Earth."

"OK, enough debating for now. We will be accelerating to sub-light in roughly," Stuart paused to examine his watch, "forty minutes. We all have our jobs." He looked over his crew; a number had concerned expressions but had not voiced the not-so-hidden thoughts. Jack Hayward, his Combat Officer, especially looked concerned. "I suggest we get to it," he finished. With that the room sprang into life, as each of his twenty crew members jumped to their well rehearsed tasks. As Jack stood to walk past him, Stuart grabbed his arm. Jack stiffened noticeably and slowly turned his eyes on Stuart. Not for the first time did Stuart have to suppress a shiver at the icy blue, cold eyes as they bored right through him. The stare was made significantly worse by the always angry red scar that formed a second, tightly pressed set of lips across Jack's throat.

"Captain?" Jack said the words carefully.

"I'm just as concerned as you are, Jack."

"Yes, sir, you should be. *Benevolent* may be fast, but she is lightly armoured and even more lightly weaponed, and she's not as manoeuvrable as you might think."

"At the first sign of danger, we get the hell out of there."

"Sir, may I be frank and speak freely?"

"Why do I think I might regret this? But yes, speak freely."

"You have history with these Hessr. Will you keep your head clear when it comes down to it?"

"I will, Jack."

"Just so you know – if you don't, I won't hesitate to do what needs doing."

CHAPTER FIVE

River straightened, wiped the tip of the soldering iron on the wet sponge and slid the hot metal into the coil. Slowly he knuckled his lower back and considered the layout in front of him. He traced the logical paths through the gates and added up the results in his mind. His vision focused into a tunnel, he could visualise the electrons flying through the gates, being diverted by their presence into alternative realities and finding their way to different conclusions. He sped along the planes of an existence that very few humans could visualise. Suddenly he snapped back into his natural consciousness.

"Yes, I think that will work," he announced to no one in particular. It had been more than a month since Stuart had left towards the next solar quadrant to go and do whatever it was that Stuart did for HEC.

River walked around his desk, approached his terminal and began to punch in his compiling sequence to execute his test programme against his circuitry. The data scrolled across the screen rapidly; he did not bother to read it. Even if he were so inclined, he would be hard pressed to keep up with the readouts. He'd get a report at the end of the compile. He lifted his jacket from the backrest of the chair and shrugged into it. A space walk was beckoning in a short bit. If his circuitry worked, he would travel a goodly distance from the Saucer to his brainchild. Two gigantic metal rings suspended in the frigid darkness of Saturn's shadow, only three degrees above absolute zero, the only energy in evidence being that of the original cosmic energy, residual from the Big Bang. For his theory to work, River needed absolutely no interference. Once he knew the pristine data, he could tweak it further.

His feet echoed a quiet patter as he padded on soft-soled slippers to the coffee maker and poured himself another mug of the black liquid. It was his last brew. The beans were out. He was not sure he would've made it this far without it. He knew the headaches would be back once he was out of his beans, but the headaches would not be a problem if the icon was green at the end of the compile.

River's confidence was high.

The scrolling text had come to a halt. Dots were repeating from left to right in a slow rhythm. The compiler was calculating the final results. River took a long sip from the mug. Slowly he lowered the mug. The screen had gone blank.

Fingers slowly released. The mug descended as if there were almost no gravitational pull towards the floor. It made contact. River could only hear the rending of ceramic as the molecules forcibly tore apart and subsequent slosh of liquid meeting solid. Reality accelerated and hit him full in the forehead. His head snapped back.

"Yes!" he screamed. "Yes! Yes! Yes! Fucking yes!"

On screen, flashed a green tick mark. Not large. The coding of the compiling software was not ostentatious as in the movies, just a small tick next to rows of black text on a white background. But that green tick could not be any larger for River. All the algorithms were correctly translated into his circuitry and the theoretical data stood up to the barrage.

"Theory is only theory, until the practical proves it correct," he recited his old lecturer.

He snatched the circuit board from the test bench and proceeded to fit it into the protective casing that he would ultimately fasten to the launch ring once he got out to there. He was rushing, he knew, but he was struggling to contain himself. Fumbling with the final screws he fastened the lid on the container, and bolted from his laboratory.

#

The ring was coming closer and closer towards him, each metre an agonising one. The closer he got the more he realised the sheer immensity of what it was that he was building. The entire Saucer would fit into the ring ten times over and with room to spare. It had to be large enough to accommodate all eventualities.

The secret was in the power source, but how exactly it worked River had yet to fully understand. It was related to dark matter colliding with matter. The Bloon, an enigmatic life form from Gliese, had bestowed the knowledge on him some months ago, but it had taken Edison in his incorrigible manner to remind him how to apply the knowledge.

He made contact with the ring with a jolt. Slowly he fastened himself to the structure before removing the container from his belt, clumsily undoing the clasps that had secured it to his suit. *All the advances, and we still have these cumbersome space suits. That will be the next thing I focus my attention on.*

Sixty tense minutes later, the circuitry was fitted and River was floating back on occasional bursts of carbon dioxide toward the waiting ship.

He entered through the small airlock and once pressure and oxygen were restored to the chamber, he was helped out of the suit by Shiori.

"Is it in place?" she quizzed him.

"Yes, Shi, if it wasn't, you think I'd be back?" he laughed.

"No, probably not. You'd run out of oxygen before you came back as a failure."

"Come, let's see what happens." He grabbed her arm and half ran toward the control room.

The control room was simply outfitted, two chairs mounted to the floor looked out through a large viewport over masses of screens, buttons and keyboards, knobs and dials. Through the viewport loomed the massive ring, still looking rough with pipes and large gaps where River would eventually have smooth coverings to protect the inner workings of his invention from stray particles and objects careening through space. To one side of the ring hovered a container ship, its arched shape missing the containers that it would normally support underneath its structure. The container ship was substantially larger than any of River's previous test objects but he didn't want to chance biological or valuable matter just yet. He had spent much of the HEC's research and development budget on objects that would never be found again, or if they were discovered and retrieved they would be of little use to anyone. The container ship was fully remotely controlled, something that Shiori specialised in. It was equipped with all manner of sensors and telemetry to measure every single piece of data they could imagine. The most important measure was distance covered in time elapsed.

"It's now or never, Shi."

"You ready?"

"Just a moment," exhaled River. He looked over the instrumentation one last time. He closed his eyes and reached out for the largest button on the console in front of him. "Engaging the Launch Accelerator."

The ring shuddered once and no more.

"Nothing?" sighed Shiori, obviously disappointed.

"What? Why?" shouted River, frustrated. He stood to check the instrumentation furthest away from him. "Power is normal and supply is steady. Why would it not come to life?"

"Wait! Look," Shiori was pointing into the centre of the ring. In the heart of the ring a globe of white energy was forming, and coalescing in a rotating beauty with almost imperceptible blue and green hues.

"It's working!" he shouted. Shiori just laughed in reply. "OK, wait until the energy has expanded all the way to the edges of the containment ring, then begin the approach of the test ship. Have you engaged all the telemetry?"

"Yes, River, of course I have," she replied, sounding slightly wounded. River was too excited and fixated on the spectacle unfolding in front of him to take notice.

The alpha-class engines ignited on the container ship and, at a low glow, pushed the ship towards the ring.

"What's the recorded speed?" questioned River.

"Three hundred kilometres per hour. Nearing Launch Accelerator, approach of event horizon imminent. In five, four, three, two…" Shiori was interrupted by a shudder to the control ship.

"What's the recorded speed!" shouted River, more in exclamation than in question.

"It's gone from the telemetry, nothing is reporting."

"How is that possible?"

"It's not there, it's gone."

"Then we've failed again."

"No, it's back, no speed, it's stationary."

"Distance?"

"Five AU."

"How is that possible, the second Launch Accelerator is nowhere near that far away?"

"Deceleration?" offered Shiori.

"Shiori, do you know what this means?" River spoke in a solemn tone.

Shiori answered equally solemnly. "Yes, River. You

have succeeded in reaching twenty times the speed of light."

CHAPTER SIX

River stood amongst his science peers in the mess hall, which had hastily been decorated with celebratory paraphernalia. Saturn as usual provided the awe-inspiring backdrop. All the professors, doctors, graduates, lackeys and general staff were on hand to witness the scene, each dressed casually and completely relaxed. The usually stuffy men and women of science had cast aside their bookish and serious natures and, having embraced their repressed wilder sides, were in high spirits as the alcohol flowed freely. Shiori especially looked resplendent; she beamed at him from a distance across the sea of faces.

Edison, holding two glasses of light sparkling wine, cleared a small circle of space in the middle of gathered crowd. He waved River over and handed him a glass. The assembled quietened down.

"A toast to scientific achievement," said Edison with his glass raised high, a round of approval following closely behind. The Professor waited for the applause to die down, without lowering his glass. "After many years of toiling, our esteemed colleague has finally brought his searching and his experimenting to a finality. A discovery. Tonight we honour you, Professor Goldstein, in our own little manner."

"Thank you, Professor," he said, accepting the toast. "I hope that my discovery will usher in a new age of exploration and discovery of other planetary systems, life forms and mineral riches."

"That it most certainly will, at twenty times the speed of light our solar system will no longer be a boundary to humanity," agreed the Professor.

A second round of applause followed, and River

began to make his way out of the limelight, nodding to faces as he walked. The attention was more than he was accustomed to and he found himself drawn to the far end of the bar-counter, where the mass of bodies was the thinnest. He leaned up against the bar, and looked over the crowd. The music had started up again, and slowly but surely the music and the alcohol got the stiff bodied scientists to begin the clumsy gyrations they classed as dancing.

A tap on his shoulder caught him off-guard, and the start released an accidental yelp.

"Can I steal you from your dream world for a moment?" Shiori asked him, leaning closer to his ear to be heard over the noise of people and background music.

"You may," grinned River.

"Thought we might share a shot of something strong?"

"Tonight, I think, we can certainly share a shot of something strong," he agreed readily, pushing the thoughts of the morning afterward to the back of his mind.

Shiori stood on her toes and leaned forwards over the bar to grab the attention of the barman, while River turned his back and surveyed the crowd of the Saucer's denizens. *It certainly is a big turnout, but then I guess this is a big deal*, he considered. "Hey, Shiori, you think we can catch up with Stuart if we build a highway towards Ganymede?"

"Slow down there, Tiger," she grinned. "For now, park that busy mind of yours and have this." She handed him a brownish shooter; it was a double.

"What's this?"

"A surprise." Her eyes were gleaming.

River took a quick sniff of the liquid, it had a sharp peppery smell. *Not offensive*. He dropped back the liquid, just as Shiori put her glass down on the counter. As he finished he found her mouth meeting his in a strong kiss. For a brief moment he fought it, but then allowed his guard down and found himself kissing her back. River had to fight for breath once they had finally separated. One part from the wave of lust the kiss had brought with it, one part from the strong concoction of liquor.

"I think we should disappear and have our own little party," he suggested.

"Oh, I like the sound of that." She grinned widely. Shiori reached over the bar while the bartender was digging around in one of the under-counter refrigerators and pinched four bottles of various, randomly selected spirits. As she grabbed one, she thrust the first two stolen bottles into River's hands, tucked the other two under her arms and led him quickly out of the rec-area and into the corridor.

The relatively short distance to his quarters was covered quickly through the urgency in their steps. While River fumbled with his key card, she opened one of the liquor bottles, took a long swig of its contents and gasped from the strength of the pure liquor. The card-reader beeped in acceptance of the key card and the door slid open. River slipped in, followed by Shiori. She handed him the bottle and he took his swig.

It was strong liquor, almost flavourless. "This stuff is vile!"

"You'll get used to it," she laughed, taking a step towards him, moving with grace. Her eyes gleamed naughtily with sexual intent. "I like your innocence, it's..." she trailed off leaving the suggestion open to simple interpretation.

River was in reality quite inexperienced, although not naive. Her approach startled him and he took an involuntary step backwards. He had stepped up against the bed, wobbling slightly from its unexpected proximity and the alcohol. Shiori took his unsteady balance to her advantage – she grabbed his shirt, pulling him slightly towards herself, then firmly pushed him back. River fell to the bed. She climbed onto the bed after him. River seemed in a blur, reacting automatically, losing himself in the heat of the moment. Shiori was well and truly in control as she removed his shirt and slacks, covering him in her kisses. For only a moment, he thought that he should be the one in control but realised he would be bumbling his way through the encounter.

A long while later, River lay in the afterglow of the experience. Shiori had grabbed the liquor bottles and sat on the foot of the bed sipping away, watching him with amusement. "It really was your first time?" she asked quizzically.

"Yes," he answered, blushing.

"Aw, look at you!" She had a playful manner, in which she bit her lip. River found the simple motion highly attractive. "Here." She handed him the bottle. It was at that point that River knew he'd regret the booze, but simply went with it.

#

River's eyes popped open, immediately regretting the action. The ceiling was spiralling away from him and then snapping back only to start the spiral anew. The whirling of the central heating sounded more like a crew of workmen trying to remove the blast doors from the main airlock right there in his room. The previous night's drinking must have been out of control. *I can't remember a damn thing, Stuart would be proud of me.* He slowly turned himself over and raised himself onto his elbow.

Next to him, half buried beneath the sheets was a creamy, silky smooth female back. *Shiori?* "Shiori?"

What he could only presume to be Shiori murmured something unintelligible. *Damn it*, he silently cursed. *Why can't I remember what happened last night? Shower, I need to shower.*

River willed himself upright, regretting the rashness of his movements and made his way towards the bathroom in a half stumbled and semi-drunken gait. He entered the small cubicle and triggered the automatic light sensors, causing the bathroom lights to leap into full brightness, practically blinding him. He felt his stomach lurch and fell towards the toilet and began to heave his last meal into the steel bowl.

It took him three attempts, each attempt causing a new wave of nausea to crash over him and forcing a regurgitative repetition, before righting himself enough to make his way into the shower. The hot water brought back a level of sanity and River stood in the shower for a good long while to give himself as much strength as possible. He finished off the rinse cycle and activated the hot air to dry off. Not bothering with brushing his hair, he quickly rinsed his mouth out with wash and stepped out into the bedroom again.

His eyes took a moment to adjust to the dimness of the bedroom after the bright glare of the bathroom. The bedroom was in a complete state of disarray, clothing was strewn all over the floor. The thick carpet, which had been a gift of his mother's when he'd moved to the Saucer, was only barely visible. Bottles of various liquors and spirits were scattered about the room, some tipped over and others standing upright but drained of their contents. Some of the coverlets from the bed seemed torn with edges tattered. Judging by the clothing on the floor, it was definitely Shiori in the bed.

Thank goodness for that, he thought wryly. *I would*

have been highly disappointed in myself if I'd ended up with someone else.

He slowly walked up to the end of the bed, smiling to himself. For a long while, he had appreciated her from afar, always thinking her to be out of reach for someone like him and now he'd ended up being with her. It felt good.

What if she's only with me because of my success? He began doubting himself. *What if I was a last option, the best of a bad selection?*

Stop it! River shook his head.

Something caught his eye. A dark spot moved against Shiori's back causing her to stir slightly and mutter something unintelligible. Hunching over, River moved closer to the dishevelled bed. The shadows over the white sheets could have played a trick on his frazzled and injured head. Gently he took the sheet that partially covered Shiori's back and lifted it gently.

"Shit! No!" he cursed aloud, against all character.

What could only be the tail of the life form that had been discovered was slowly disappearing into Shiori's back, its head not visible. A tiny sliver of blood was running down the groove of the spine and over along the side of the lower back arch, staining the white sheet. Shiori seemed to be in no pain.

Forgetting his hangover, River grabbed his slacks from the floor and jumping into them, through a kind of hobble made his way to the door to find some help.

#

River flew down the corridor in search of someone who would help. Most of the Saucer was still fast asleep or withdrawn. He left the living quadrant and entered the engineering quad. There was always activity to be found in the engineering quadrant.

"Jason! Quick, I need your help," he called out. Jason was a big and slightly slow witted engineer who operated docking columns. Since capital ships seldom made the long journey out to the Saucer, he was mostly used for stacking crates with the light hand-operated forklifts. The menial task suited him to a tee.

The big man turned and blinked in wonder at River. "Professor Goldstein?"

"Quick, it's Shiori. She's injured, bleeding, some kind of creature…" he was out of breath and incoherent. He could see that he was not getting through to him. "Quickly, just come with, I need help carrying her to the med-bay."

"OK, OK. I'm coming." He finally seemed to react.

The two of them raced back down the corridor towards the living quad. Jason had greater physical prowess than River and started to outpace him, barrelling past River's quarters on towards Shiori's. River had to call him back.

The big man looked confused when he approached River's door. "What's Doctor Wu doing in here?" The answer came slowly to his eyes and his mouth dropped open.

"Never mind that, Jason, just help me." River opened the door without his key card, having not locked it on his way out, and stepped into his room. The room was in the same state in which he'd left it. Only Shiori was missing.

"Prof.? Is this some kind of joke? Are you trying to brag about something that didn't happen?"

"Where…?" He was confused. The room looked exactly how he'd left it. He could even make out the place where she had lain just moments before. "The blood!"

"Blood?"

"Yes, she was bleeding from her back, where the

life form was burrowing into her."

"Life form? Prof., you're not making sense."

"Shiori – she was here. The missing life form, it was burrowing into her back. Just here," he tried to show the location on his own back, twisting his arm behind his back. All that this bouncing around achieved was greater confusion.

"But Shiori isn't here, Prof. Why don't we go and see if she's up? Maybe she can clarify what's going on?"

River paused, and eventually agreed. "Yes, yes, of course..." Jason led the way out, River following lost in thought.

The distance to Shiori's quarters was not too far; she was only ten doors further down. Jason rung the announcement ringer, and shortly afterward the door slid open. Shiori stood in the doorway, hair wet, wearing denim jeans and a white untucked, loose, overlarge T-shirt. She was towel drying her long, jet-black hair. "Good morning Professor Goldstein, Jason. How can I help this morning?"

"Shiori, are you all right?" launched River. The expression she gave him stopped him well short. She did not look comfortable with the familiarity.

"Of course I'm all right. Why wouldn't I be?"

"You were bleeding from your back, when I came out of the shower. I rushed to go get help and..." She interrupted him with a raised hand, cocking her head to the side in an offended gesture.

"Shower? Are you insinuating that we spent the night together, Professor?" she said with a haughty laugh. The laugh cut deeply.

"Shiori, what are you saying?"

Jason spoke up. "I'm sorry, Doctor Wu. I can see that Professor Goldstein is being a harassment. I'm sorry for the disturbance..."

"Wait a minute, Shiori, I clearly saw your back." River made to lift her untucked shirt but she stepped back and Jason stepped in to intercept the attempt.

"Professor Goldstein, I don't think that is a wise move," said the big man firmly. River attempted to say more, but Jason continued speaking over his shoulder whilst moving River away from the doorway. "I'm sorry about this, Doctor Wu."

Shiori shut the door with no further word, leaving River out in the cold.

CHAPTER SEVEN

"This obsession of yours with Doctor Wu is unbecoming, unprofessional and utterly pathetic," said Edison calmly, quietly and with far too much contempt in his voice than River would have been able to digest at the best of times. But nevertheless, here he sat, inside Edison's office, all his glory surrounding his big achievement gone; dried up just like the first rains on the saltpans back in his homeland on Earth. "Do you think you are the first person to think you landed the big prize? You got drunk, passed out and dreamed up a fantasy that wasn't real. Get over it, move on and stop pestering the good doctor."

"I know what I saw, Professor."

"Professor Goldstein, persist in this and I will have you removed from this facility."

"Are you threatening me?"

"Oh no, I'm not threatening." The irritating man seemed vastly amused by the statement. "I'm not threatening you at all. I'm telling you. River, I'm going to be as frank as I possibly can." The old scientist did not wait for any kind of acknowledgement or permission, he simply continued. "You are talented and intelligent, there is no doubt about that, but you are not wise. You are so very far from wise, it's painful to observe. There is a very large part of me that is tempted to let you continue on this self-destructive path you seem to have chosen for yourself. In the competitive world of scientific discovery, it would be the strategic move on my part. But with the small part of compassion I have for you, through respect of your abilities as peer, perhaps at a push, as a comrade, I recognise that would be a waste. You have too much

47

still to give to the scientific community, don't spoil it all now because of a fantasy induced by too much drink and a snubbing."

"But, sir…" River stopped, knowing that he had lost the argument long ago. "It all felt so real," he finished quietly. "And Shiori has not been herself since that morning. I *know* what I saw. The life form has disappeared, none of us can find it. Even the bio-scanners are turning up nil. I *saw* it burrowing into her back. She has changed. I'm not the only one who has noticed. People speak about her changes, only none will put it to the test. I'm telling you, Professor, if you check her back you'll see a scar, wound, scab, something…"

"All of what you say is based purely on your word. As a man, you have no weight to throw at this. She is a woman who has done nothing wrong and is entitled to her privacy. At your insistence, I have asked her if we could check her back. She refused, entirely in her right."

River could only nod; everything the Professor was saying was true.

"River, please, just let it be, or face the full consequences of a harassment charge. And have no false pretences, she will level one against you."

"Sir, in that case, I must ask for a transfer from the Saucer."

Edison nodded. *He has been expecting this request,* the realisation hit River. *Can I really blame him for expecting that? Most people wouldn't be able to face the humiliation.*

"Where will you transfer to?"

"I was thinking I might switch to a less scientific role. I wish to work on the highway deployment project."

"Ah, yes, see your brainchild deployed. I will write

to the committee requesting your reassignment."

River rose from his chair opposite the Professor's desk. The Professor stood in accompaniment shortly afterward. The handshake was completed, extended across the desk. "Thank you for your accommodation during my tenure here at Research Facility Six Oh One."

"Good luck in your future endeavours," said the Professor, turning his head away as he dug into his pockets to find his handkerchief. He hurriedly blew his nose, wiping away what seemed like a greenish slime.

"Professor, I'm not a medical doctor, but mucus of that colour cannot be healthy. You should have that looked at."

"It's nothing, just a small cold." He waved River's suggestion away irritably. "You have things to address, let me not keep you any longer."

#

Casting one last look over the two-room quarters he had inhabited for almost six full years, River ran his key card over the reader and let the door slide shut. The room held few happy memories for him, he had spent very little time in the austere chambers and the time he had spent in there had been lonely. The one time he did spend time with company had turned out to be a vivid figment of his imagination.

He handed the key card over the HEC security officer. "Here you go, the last slice of RF601 property in my possession. I think I've lingered here long enough."

The security officer only nodded and turned so that he would be walking just a step behind River. *From scientific delight to legal liability*, he thought cynically.

None of the Saucer's inhabitants were on-hand to

see him off, as they had all been in a frenzy about something. The HEC-SEC representatives had arrived on a larger interdictor-class capital ship, the *Agamemnon*, one of the largest capital ships in the HEC fleet. The interdictor was capable of operating for long periods of time away from any kind of space platform or base. It carried many thousands of personnel, from scientists to engineers, from cooks to combatants. *Agamemnon* had been a long distance out from Sol and was finally returning from Gliese, and had been nominated by HEC-HQ to begin setting up the Highway from Saturn to Earth. There were two primary reasons for this: firstly, the *Agamemnon* was one of the fastest capital ships in the fleet, secondly, due to its size it was able to produce and keep an inventory of the actual components needed, as the ship travelled between the locations where the Highway junctions would be placed.

The path to the long docking column was deserted, almost as if his former colleagues had taken pains to avoid him. And before long he was heading towards the massive airlock. Parts of the *Agamemnon*'s hull were visible from the docking collar, since it was actually larger than the entry portal. Not that any ships were larger than the *Agamemnon*, but River supposed it had to do with the fact that the designers were constantly looking forward to possible changes and tried to build things to accommodate as much change as possible. A large docking column could easily be modified to fit something smaller, but large scale changes would be needed to accommodate something of a larger nature.

In the entry stood two officers, one of them clearly the Admiral, the other looking to be his First Officer. The Admiral was a man of large build, stocky and old. His face was marked with stress lines. The man had clearly experienced much in his time. The First Officer looked middle aged at first glance. He was well groomed and showed little sign of ageing. A closer look revealed the man to be far older, his true age betrayed in his eyes, which revealed even greater experience than the Admiral's.

River stepped over the threshold into the *Agamemnon* and was greeted by the Admiral. "Admiral R. Bennett; and this is Flight Commander S. Bamford, my second-in-command on ship. We have heard much about you, Professor Goldstein."

"Hopefully the better things, Admiral."

"Of course." The Admiral inclined his head, betraying that the information imparted had been primarily negative. "We wish to be off as soon as possible to commence our work. We have the benefit of the first two junctions to get us as far as the outer moons of Jupiter, but thereafter many light minutes of normal flight await us."

"Certainly, the quicker I can get settled and begin with my new work the better." They began to walk down the corridor into the deeper sections of the capital ship. Just beyond where they had been speaking stood three crewmen who snapped to attention as they passed. The Flight Commander waved them into action as they passed. River could only presume that the process of closing up the airlock would begin and that the capital ship would be pulling from dock soon.

"Bamford will show you to your quarters, he will be your effective CO since you don't fit into the martial ranks, per se. I saw from your file you are classified a lieutenant with regards to on-deck authority and general benefits or recognition?"

"I believe so, sir, though I haven't specifically paid any attention to that due to my time on the Saucer being highly secluded."

"Well, on board the *Agamemnon* that rank will be

highly important, and you will find it coming into play frequently. I trust you will act as your rank dictates and how decorum demands."

The real crunch of the rank inquiry, my experience with Shiori, will not be so easily forgotten, it seems, thought River bitterly. "Of course not, sir. I intend to be the model of decorum and complete my new tasks dutifully."

The old man nodded as if he expected no less than what he had just heard. By that time they had just made it to a crossing of corridors. "Bamford will take you the rest of the way to the sleeping quarters. You will be sharing a cabin with another lieutenant. You will at least not be in the general quarters with hundreds of junior enlisted crewmen. I have things to attend to on the bridge. Good day, Lieutenant Goldstein."

"Thank you, Admiral."

"This way," said Flight Commander Bamford as he strode down the opposite direction to which the Admiral had headed. River had to hurry to keep step with his new direct superior.

Another cold and detached boss, he sighed inwardly.

#

After a brief tour of his section and introduction to a whole sea of new faces, River found himself in a cramped chamber. A single bunk, a tiny little desk a mere two feet from the edge of it, with a narrow locker beside the desk. The walls of his chamber were no more than five feet apart. The whole ceiling was a source of light, which could be dimmed or brightened as desired.

A claustrophobic place this is, compared with my old quarters, he thought to himself. *Time to move on,*

River.

He stowed his belongings away and tried to recall the names of the faces he had been introduced to, but couldn't recall anything. A voice croaked from a speaker, somewhere hidden away. He suspected it to be the voice of the First Mate, or the Admiral.

"All crew, please secure yourself for full acceleration in thirty minutes."

"And the new chapter starts now," he said loudly to no one in particular, a smile etched across his face.

Part 2

Map of Core Systems, 3053-10

CHAPTER EIGHT

Two years into the deployment of the Highway and most of the solar system was covered by a hash of routes. Four routes, two to either side of the sun, running parallel and at ninety degrees to each other allowed one to reach any of the destinations in Sol relatively quickly.

River had been itching for the moment that he could step away from his project's deployment. He hadn't been involved with all four routes, only the first. After having seen the first one implemented, he had become a member of a crack-team deployed to address any major deployment issues that needed to be resolved before they became major stumbling-blocks to the overall project timelines.

After almost a decade away from home, River was now standing at the hatch that opened up onto a corridor. This corridor would lead him into one of the many spacevator halls that hung in static orbit around Mother Earth. Back in the early twenty-first century mankind had realised that using solid-fuel rockets was an inefficient way of beating gravity and escaping the atmosphere. It took many more centuries before an alternative became a subsidised service available to anyone. Now a grand total of twenty space-elevators reached up into the heavens and moved up to a hundred passengers per five day trip. Ironically, the longest part of a journey to Titan was now the trip through the Earth's safety shield and to good old terra firma.

The hall was busy, with a small horde of people milling around either waiting for transport from the spacevator or for transport down to Earth. River was cutting it fine, timing-wise. The transport he'd used from the space station, where the *Agamemnon* was in dock, was intended for Earth-departing passengers. Pushing through the crowd of newly arrived people, River only just made it on board the elevator as the doors were closing.

He was travelling lightly. Having been on a research facility for many years and then on a military vessel his every human need had been taken care of and without any retail around he had not accumulated any possessions aside from those in this little suitcase and the clothes on his back.

The elevator was nothing like the simple nine-by-nine elevators normally used to get bodies from one level to the next. The spacevators were immense structures similar to hotels, rated according to the same star-scale as traditional hotels. A trip could be had in utter luxury or in cramped class. River, lacking funds, was headed for a basic, two-star spacevator.

One thing all spacevators shared, aside from the obvious beds and food halls, were facilities in which the human body could be subjected to intense training if the stay away from Earth had been longer than three Earth-months. The human body lost bone density with extended absence from the $1g$ that the Earth provided. In River's case, in the time aboard the Saucer with replicated $1g$ he would have been spared the training, but the *Agamemnon*, like all capital ships, had only a $0.7g$ gravity system.

He worked his way through the lobby of the spacevator and towards F-corridor, which led to his room and which, according to the brochure, would be far roomier than his accommodation aboard the *Agamemnon*.

A broom closet is the lap of luxury compared with that narrow cubicle, he thought wryly.

To reach the F-corridor he had to bypass the central

food-cum-bar area that sported a transparisteel bottom. Through this clear bottom, one was afforded a glorious view of the planet as it descended through the darker outer layers of the atmosphere. It was a sight to behold, and one he had almost forgotten. The descent was supposedly more spectacular than the ascent, since the heat of the re-entry created some impressive light orchestras along the underside of the spacevator.

The bar-counter was wrapped around the middle of the spacevator, also made of transparisteel. It had a doughnut shape, and through the middle ran a high tensile cable, more akin to a pillar, wider at the zenith than at the base. It was a marvel of early engineering that had yet to be revised in almost five hundred years since the first version had been completed by the Chinese.

If it weren't for the transparent centre, and a visual reminder of the cable running through the middle, one would never notice the commencement of the descent. In the vacuum there was no gravity to give a sensation of the structure moving.

The news was showing on one of the screens suspended just above the bar-counter. Someone was interested in what was being said and was asking for the volume to be increased. The bartender obliged.

"…thirteen months since its disappearance, and the subsequent escalation of open warfare between GSOL and HEC, the *Benevolent* has been found on Elara. The hull is said to have sustained heavy damage and no bodies have been located as yet. HEC officials have not commented on whether the *Benevolent* was destroyed by GSOL attack or whether the *Benevolent* was simply damaged as a result of poor captaincy. Nevertheless, the incident has been the catalyst for escalated war activities, which still shows no signs of abating. We are joined by…"

River stopped listening and looked down towards Earth, stunned by the news he'd just heard.

Stuart was one of the best pilots he had ever known. He was cautious to a fault and highly dutiful. River could not believe that Stuart would have been reckless and neither could River believe that his friend would have taken the *Benevolent* into a dangerous situation that he could otherwise have avoided.

"Something has happened to Stuey. And I'm going to find out what," he declared to the room. No one responded.

#

River had been eating a late breakfast when the stewards began making their rounds to inform the passengers of the impending arrival. They were given thirty minutes to find and secure their belongings and to sequester themselves to their rooms. The corridors and common areas all needed to be devoid of people for safety reasons. Statistically, the spacevators were highly safe, but whenever a public service was concerned the safety was always paramount.

I'm certain that cargo spacevators are nowhere near as tight on security, thought River cynically to himself as he entered his small room. He had splurged a bit of his savings to have a room with a window. He could have saved himself a fair amount of cash if he had gone with one of the rooms on the inner side of the corridor, those had no windows and were a little smaller due to the circular shape of the room. The outer rooms had a large footprint, but curved upwards at the window and so had less usable floor space than the inner chambers. The design came with a safety benefit: it was impossible to stand right up against the window due to the curvature.

The initial descent seemed quicker. As the spacevator neared the Earth, the blue curvature disappeared and the light just outside his windows moved from the deep darkness of space into a deep blue hue and rapidly brightened. Within a short period of time Earth dominated the view and space was lost to his vision. Thereafter the descent became slow and boring. River quickly reached the conclusion that he could have saved himself a fair amount of money and gone for a room without a view.

The five days were torturous for River. Without something substantial to immerse himself in he was lost to a routine that did not fit his usual busy self. His days were filled with three mundane meals whilst watching whatever was being displayed on the public channels, or wandering back and forth between his room, the canteen and gym. He purposefully stayed away from any alcohol due to his experiences with Shiori. His idle mind was plagued by memories of watching the life form burrow itself into Shiori's back.

I must have imagined it, nothing of such a nature could truly exist, he kept telling himself in a feeble attempt at dispelling his unease.

So it happened that the public announcement of the spacevator's imminent arrival on the surface of Earth came with a welcome and energetic smile. River was among the first to disembark. He worked himself through the milling masses of people towards the exits of the terminal.

It was raining in New London. It mostly rained on Earth. Since the melting of the polar ice caps some thousand years ago, the atmosphere had become highly damp. Thunderstorms only formed out over the ocean, and over land it simply drizzled constantly, never getting any heavier than a firm downpour. Annually, most cities experienced at most four weeks of sunshine.

During those weeks, all commerce and activity came to a grinding halt as the population of overcrowded Earth would abstain from any kind of labour and simply bask in the sun in relaxation or in merriment.

Not having experienced rain in decades, River stepped out from underneath the awning that shielded the entrance to the terminal and allowed the rain to soak him thoroughly. The rain tasted sweet as he allowed the water to cascade along his facial features and pool in his opened mouth. To anyone watching him, of which there were a few, he would have looked like a case for an institution. He enjoyed the feeling of abandonment for only a moment longer before composing himself and looking around.

At the pavement stood a woman, holding an umbrella in one hand and a small sign in the other. The sign had his name scrawled all over it. She must have noticed his gaze and the recognition in his eyes, for she stepped towards him.

"Professor River Goldstein?"

"Yes, I am Professor Goldstein," he answered cautiously.

"Hi, I'm Jennifer Baldwin, Channel One News." When River showed no recognition, she added. "We arranged to have an interview about your amazing, life changing discovery and invention. The Galactic Highway." Jennifer was beaming.

"Oh, yes, of course. How silly of me," he answered with a sheepish chuckled. River found himself to be made suddenly quite nervous by the attention. Unbidden memories flooded back into his consciousness of the last time an attractive woman had showered praise and adulation on him. Shiori. "Are we doing the interview here?" he asked, confused, looking around.

"No, of course not," she laughed. "We are here to

collect you, and bring you past the station, where we'll do the interview in dry comfort. Thereafter, our driver will drop you off wherever it was that you were going to be going."

The driver took River's satchel off him and placed it into the boot, and with little fanfare they departed. The driver activated the switching function, which engaged the magnetic repulsers, lifting the car off the ground and gently guiding it towards the magnetic track embedded into the tar. Slowly the car began to move forwards and joined in with the steady flow of traffic. The highways of Earth required little driving skill as the magnetic tracks allowed the vehicles to move forwards in perfect synchronicity. The speed of travel was dictated by congestion and accidents were a thing of the past. Only system failure could cause disruption, and that was a highly rare occurrence.

A short twenty minute commute had them pulling up to a narrow spire of a building that rose high up above them, but also dipped well below the raised platform they stood on. New London was a multi-tiered city, with many layers, the lowest of which had none of the magnetic roads and highways of the upper level, but rather canals with little long-pole boats for commuting. The sea level had risen strongly over the last thousand years.

\#

"We are live in five, four, three," stated the producer, switching to hand signals from two to one, then pointing at Jennifer.

"Welcome to another edition of 'One-on-One' with Jennifer. Tonight, I am with Professor Goldstein, a young and brilliant mind who has over the last two years seen his latest discovery deployed throughout our solar system," she said to the camera. Turning to face him, she continued. "Hello Professor, thank you for joining me."

River nervously looked directly at the camera and got an admonishing look from the producer, so he snapped his eyes back to the woman. "Hi, it's a pleasure."

"Professor, I must admit, that when I read about your invention I was a little lost at how exactly it works, but it's safe to say that this will change the way we travel?"

"Not just that, Ms Baldwin, it will change life as we know it."

"In what way?"

"Well, getting from here to Titan in under six minutes is quite a difference from the six months of a few years ago."

"From six months to six minutes – some would say that's impossible. So how did you achieve this, Professor?"

"Well, it was a matter of understanding the forces at play and then creating an anomaly in the space/time continuum. I harness that energy in a binder of sorts and channel an outlet for that energy in a specific direction."

Jennifer began to get a lost expression on her face, so River held back with the rest of the scientific description. "I use massive metal rings called accelerators to accelerate a vessel up to the size of an interdictor capital ship up to effectively twenty times the speed of light."

"I'm no scientist, Professor, but isn't the common understanding that nothing can travel faster than the speed of light?"

"In a straight line, yes."

"In a straight line?"

"Yes, Ms Baldwin, in a straight line. But what I'm actually doing is bringing a location a number of light seconds further away much closer for only a couple of split seconds, then travelling that short distance before doing it again. And in effect creating twenty times the speed of light without ever truly accelerating up to that speed. Which is why I required multiple accelerators to build up the Highway."

"Fascinating, and this actually works?"

"If it didn't, I would not have spent two years deploying the technology," he joked, though she didn't seem to see that with the same humour as he did.

"So when will this Highway be open to free commerce?"

River hesitated a little; it was something he had never thought to ask. Nor had he ever thought to put any regulations in place. He had figured that the higher-ups at the HEC would have had that figured out. "I don't actually know. That all depends on the Confederacy."

"So are we to assume the use will be purely military?"

"I didn't say that, and I think that is speculation. The Highway was designed by me to be used for all mankind."

"But you have no say, by your own admission, in how it will be used."

"Look, Ms Baldwin, I'm a scientist and I was working for the Confederacy at the time, so the designs belong to the Confederacy in part and in part they belong to me as well. The Confederacy has always had the best in mind for everyone and I don't see that changing."

"Uh-huh," she answered, while she flipped through her notes.

"You said you used to work for the Confederacy.

After such a momentous discovery, why would you leave their employment?"

"I'd rather not talk about that."

"Sounds like there are something's going on behind the scenes, Professor. So where to from here?"

"For me? I'm going to take a bit of a time out and see where to next. I have some ideas," he answered, doing his best to sound confident of the fact. Perhaps unknowingly, or perhaps completely according to plan, the reporter and talk show host had planted some worries in his mind. Snapping back to reality, he noticed that she had been talking to the camera again and before he knew it the bright overhead lights had dimmed and the crew were rushing forward.

Jennifer stood briefly, and held out her hand. "Thank you, Professor. I hope things in life work out for you. Excuse me for being short, but we need to continue filming the rest of the show." She sat back down and he was herded out of the studio.

The experience left him feeling surreal and incorporeal.

CHAPTER NINE

River stood in a gloomy corridor in front of a steel door with the number 206 listed above it. His old apartment, just a couple of blocks from his old university, New Cambridge. The irony that New Cambridge was in New London still amused him. He held his ring finger to the biometric reader and after a short validation sequence the door slid to the side and permitted him entry.

The lights in the corridor didn't automatically activate since River had powered down all the systems in the apartment, not wanting to run up any kind of exorbitant accounts during his decade-long absence. The place smelt mouldy, damp and unwelcoming.

After a short delay, while he searched for the mains switches, he quickly brought all the systems online and soon had the ventilation system pumping fresh air into the various chambers. He busied himself for a couple of hours removing protective sheeting, vacuuming up dust with the centralised vacuum system and opening the few windows he had. He crammed all his washing into the washer and set it to a long and thorough wash, dry and decreasing cycle. Then he popped out for fresh supplies while that was in progress.

In a world so far advanced, the mundane chores had remained relatively unchanged for millennia.

Being a bachelor, River felt little guilt stocking up mainly on snacks and ready-to-eat meal packs and soon enough he was home with his cooker heating a R2E meal.

The interview had left him shaken, compounded with the news report that claimed his friend's recklessness to be the cause of escalated war activities. The populace of New London was uneasy, he had felt it out in the streets and in the stores. People were afraid of war coming to Earth. There were rumours of Hessr attacks on other moons or planets; Ceres was often rumoured to have been affected by some kind of attack. The tensions were high, that much was for sure.

Only River was having a hard time believing it.

Stuart is so particular about where and how he flies, he would never fly into a situation he had no chance of coming out of. Unless he was ambushed.

River stopped in his pacing. The cooker alarm was beeping in the distance from the kitchen, but he ignored it.

"Stuart was ambushed, but by whom? His instructions were secret and encoded by HEC command. GSOL would never have known he was coming!"

With quick strides he reached his communicator panel in the lounge, one of the only two rooms with a window. His view was limited though. He could only just make out the large square between the sides of three large residential tenements. He scrolled through his list of contacts until he found the Confederacy office for his sector. He dialled them up.

"Human Earth Confederacy, North Sector, New London. How may I direct your call?" answered an automated, recorded voice.

"Please connect me to Admiral Bennett, *CCS Agamemnon.*"

"The *Agamemnon* is still in dock and available. If you are of the HEC, please provide your identification number using the keypad on your communicator."

River punched in the twenty-five digit ID and waited patiently.

After what seemed an eternity, the Admiral came on the line. "Lieutenant Goldstein, I thought I'd heard the last of you."

"Sorry to bother you, sir, but I have only a single request of you."

"Out with it, I'm a busy man, and we are soon to be on our way again."

"Sir, I would like to run something by you and see if you agree with my thinking. You seem a reasonable man and I want to see if my thoughts are purely imagined or if there is possibly a seed of substance."

There was a long pause, which prompted River to doubt technology. "Hello, are you still there?"

"Yes, yes, carry on then."

"Are you familiar with the *Benevolent,* sir?"

"Yes, I am. The *Benevolent* is the missing ship, presumed destroyed, suspected catalyst of the heightened war tension and the reason we're out of dock so quickly again. What of it?"

"Well, the captain of the *Benevolent* is a long-time friend of mine and I question the manner in which the ship went missing. Captain Slate and I were together on the Saucer…"

"Saucer?"

"Sorry, that's the name by which RF601 was known to us. Captain Slate and I were together on RF601 when he received his instructions to fly out to Ganymede space where he would receive his next orders. I question why an order like that would come through; the *Benevolent* was a deep space recognisance craft not designed for dog fights or direct assault. Captain Slate followed the orders, but I could tell from his mood that he knew he was flying into a trap."

Again there was long silence. This time River chose not to rush or interrupt the Admiral's thinking. So he waited a while and then continued his thoughts aloud so that the Admiral could absorb his reasoning.

"Sir, my problem is this. The way I know Captain Slate, from years flying craft together in Old Texas, is that when he suspected trickery, he would make sure he would get an opportunity to scan or check his destination for a trap. I cannot believe that he would be caught unawares, unless he was betrayed by someone he trusted."

The Admiral mmm'd quietly into the speaker, then spoke. "I should probably not be saying this, but the events as you describe them do warrant a closer look and there are some recent orders and activities happening in the Confederacy that are strange. But our lives as soldiers are such that we do not question the orders of our superiors, which goes for you as it does for me. I will have nothing to do with this and do not contact me about this again. But I will leave you with this one piece of advice and this one piece of assistance.

"There is a retired commodore of the Confederacy Secret Service. He will listen more closely to you and might choose to help you, but I warn you he doesn't take to strangers easily. He lives in Constantinople; I will transfer his contact card to you. I suggest you visit in person, he's not too fond of digital communication.

"Lastly, be careful. Be very, very careful. You are entering a world that you might not want to be involved with."

#

River stepped off the continental ferry and into a relatively quiet port. The few people that were about paid him no mind and were not milling around in organised chaos, as was the way of most ports. The contact card that he had been sent had listed a street address, and so River had looked up directions before leaving his apartment two days ago. Earthbound public transport was no more efficient than it had been a thousand years ago. Most of the advances had happened in space and on other planets. The traditional home of the humans was still the big civilisation anchor.

Constantinople's architecture was a throwback to the old days of early third century, but combining all the modern features of the thirty-first century. This meant that buildings had flat-top roofs with eves, cornices, columns and domes according to old Turkish styles, but were designed from transparent steel, which acted as solar panels, as windows and as structural walls.

Most of the transparisteel was set to 'opaque' as River made his way along the street sides, a standard practice in most cities. Only the wealthy tended to allow their privacy loose and not hide behind facades of steel. Constantinople at least chose a variety of colours, rather than the forbidding concrete grey that New London used. Some buildings had sandy brick colouration, or mimicked the old brick and cement patterns.

The city was a maze of undocumented little side roads and alleys that bisected and criss-crossed all over the city and it took River a long time to finally find the square that the contact card had listed. A small coffee shop overlooked the square, diagonally across from the commodore's address. With the drizzle, River was loath to huddle underneath some narrow overhang and so he got himself a table, a coffee and a slice of quiche, then settled down to watch for signs of life.

As dusk settled, lights ignited in the windows and River recognised a dark shape move about closing curtains.

Curtains, how old school.

River paid the bill and crossed the square. The drizzle had turned heavier and was now a steady flow.

By the time he reached the front door, he was soaked through. He rang the bell and waited. He turned around and looked about, and noticed a cloaked man standing directly across the square. The man quickly slipped up an alley. A camera was mounted to the lamppost on the walk way and it had swivelled to focus on River. He looked up at it and waved. He heard the door open and turned around.

"Who are you?" demanded a grizzled and burly looking old man.

"Hi, my name is River Goldstein, sir. I have come to ask for your opinion."

"Go away, if you know what's best for you." And with that the door was slammed shut.

River stood stupefied on the doorstep, not knowing what to make of the cold reception. Knowing that he would be at an impasse if he didn't at least speak a little with the retired veteran, he persistently rang the bell again and waited. He was about to ring again, when the door opened.

"You can say three words, before I shoot you."

"Bennett sent me!"

"That will do, come in." The door swung open wide, and River stepped in to see the old man setting a twenty-seventh century arc-blaster aside. They were nasty weapons that fired arcs of electrically charged chrome bullets. The electricity would fry out any kind of electronic device that it made contact with in addition to punching through most armour plating; steel plating would simply conduct the voltage and amplify the damage.

The man led the way down a corridor after shutting and locking the door. They passed a room filled with monitors showing various alleys, corridors and rooms before arriving in his kitchen. He motioned to a rickety looking aluminium chair at a small table.

"I'm making tea. You want?"

"No thank you, sir."

"Anything else? Whisky? Cane?"

River couldn't help but laugh. "No thanks, sir. Need my wits about me."

"Fine. So what does Bennett want?"

"Admiral Bennett doesn't want anything, sir. It's me that wants something. Admiral Bennett simply suggested you'd know how to help."

The commodore was surveying him with a critical eye and said nothing, prompting River to continue on with his request. River relayed his suspicions about the orders that Stuart had flown to Ganymede to obey, not leaving out a single detail, and adding that from River's experience, Stuart would have flown at normal speed the final week to make sure that he could be at full alert. When he finished, the commodore sat across from him simply nursing his black, unsweetened tea.

"It's those damn infectors, I tell you."

"Sir?"

"Oh, you can stop with the titles and the politeness. Just call me Tom."

"OK, sir, er, Tom."

"I'm going to tell you a little theory I subscribe to, me and many others out there. It sounds farfetched, but no one has been able to disprove it to date, nor, sadly, prove it."

River sat back, intrigued.

"Humans have had dictators, war mongers, tyrants and terrorists for millennia. Before the birth of Christ, before time memorial, history describes each possessing similar qualities, other traits that are just too uncanny and identical to be of any kind of coincidence. Through DNA, RNA and other reconstructive methods, we have even been able to recreate the actual corpses of these various characters.

"Every single one of them carried a fist sized lump of scar tissue between their shoulder blades. Every single one of them had a nervous twitch somewhere. Genghis Khan a shoulder twitch, Hitler from the WW2 a shaking and constantly rotating hand, Tony the Carrier from the Guild Wars had a twitching eye. That's just to name a few. Then to top it off, they all have almost permanent mucous discharges from their nostrils.

"Scar tissue like that can only come from something being buried underneath the skin, from a skin rupture or a deep flesh cut. We believe that something alien infects these kinds of people, for what purpose I don't know. But I believe that they are the cause for the greatest wars in history. I believe the Hessr to be innocent of these crimes we attribute them; we have never captured one in the act. It's always by media relay.

"I got discharged, dishonourably, because of this theory, but I stick to it."

River sat stunned. Visions of the life form burrowing into Shiori's back kept flooding through his mind.

"Boy, you OK? You look like you've seen a ghost?"

"I'm... I'm OK, sir."

"Tom."

"Huh?"

"My name's not sir, it's Tom."

"Oh, sorry," River hesitated. "Sir. I believe you. I used to be a professor on the Saucer. Research Facility 601."

"I know of the Saucer. The best scientists go there. The ones that will make a difference. The ones who are working on technology that can be dangerous in the wrong hands."

"Well, a life form was brought to the facility for

73

research. It was in cryostasis. We believed it to be dead. When we thawed it, it escaped."

"Uh-huh."

"We couldn't find it. In the meantime, I managed to conclude my research into my space/time folding waypoints. The morning after my celebration in honour of my work, I witnessed the same life form burrow itself into my lady friend's back. Just between the shoulder blades. Exactly where you describe this scar tissue to be."

"My god! You might be only person alive ever to have witnessed this. I have so many questions."

"And we don't have much time. Something big is happening, I just don't know what. But I think my friend's ambush is at the heart of it."

"OK, OK. One thing, we believe the Hessr to be immune, or unaffected. Due to the war, and the general antipathy between human and Hessr, this fact has never been conclusively verified. But, we have enough evidence to support this assumption."

"I have to find my friend. And I need to prove that Shiori was infected by this life form."

"Why? What will that prove?"

"That I'm not mad. But that's not as important as me finding my friend."

"Who says he's even alive? They haven't found him, and they found his ship destroyed."

"Stuart is alive. I know it. He wouldn't have gone down so easily. And if these life forms are behind all the wars in history, I want to stop them."

"I do agree with you, destroying your friend's ship doesn't fit any possible Hessr motive," thought the old man aloud. "But boy, you're no hero. Leave this up to the professionals. You're a scientist, not some guns-blazing trooper. Why don't you just go to Bennett and get him to sort it out?"

"For the same reason you got discharged. They obviously got the top rankers. Same as they went for Hitler and the like. Admiral Bennett is in the system, he'll be powerless. It falls to us."

"In that case, I wish you best of luck. I can't help, I'm too old for this. Just watch your back. Now that you've been here, you'll be watched."

CHAPTER TEN

River elected to not stay in the hotel that he had arranged for himself, having found the retired commodore on the day of his arrival. The discussion about the parasitic life form had instilled a sense of urgency and fear. Urgency to stop a war and a level of terror the human race might not have faced before. Fear due to the truth in the commodore's words. River was no hero. He was a simple scientist who had inadvertently made a momentous discovery. He secretly felt that his discovery had been pure happenstance and that sooner or later someone more renowned would have made the discovery anyways. The mere fact that he had not thought of the implications of his invention highlighted the fact that he was no one special.

Addressing this did fall to him though. If the commodore were to be believed, then River was the only person to have ever witnessed the parasite burrow itself into a human body. Why it chose Shiori he could not fathom. *What role could she play that would advance their cause? She only assisted me. Unless it was after me, and I escaped it by showering?*

Lost in thought he arrived back at the platform and went to stand in the queue at the check-in counter. His ticket had a variable return date, and he would be able to make the next continental ferry back to New London. The queue was moving slowly, there were many families ahead of him in the queue and their check-ins with their multiple suitcases and bodies took longer.

He spotted what he thought was the man who had been watching him earlier outside the commodore's house. This time, the man was seated on a bench that overlooked the queue, he was reading a paper and looked the complete stereotype of an observer trying not to be noticed.

Should I go over there and challenge him? I'll lose my place in the queue and time is of the essence.

River chose to remain in the queue, since it had filled up behind him and he still wished to make it back on the next ferry. As he reached the counter he noticed the man stand up, fold his newspaper under his arm and then walk towards to the security gates. River's attention was forced to the lady behind the counter.

"Hi, I wish to travel back on the next ferry."

"Do you have a ticket already?"

"Yes." He slipped the ticket under the security glass.

"I won't be able to accommodate you on the class you've booked. We have a full booking for set seats. I can put you down one class or you can pay a little extra to move up a class."

"Shouldn't you move me up a class in compensation?"

"The terms of a variable ticket don't allow this."

"OK fine, a class down will have to do. Though I expect once I'm on board first economy will have spare seats."

"Anything to declare, or baggage to check in?"

"No, just my carry-on bag."

"You have nothing sharp, explosive or dangerous in there?"

"No, nothing."

"Here is your ticket, seat 98H. Boarding ramp B3. We depart in one hour."

"Thank you."

The trip through the security check went smoothly and quickly, as did the trip to his boarding ramp. The ramp was still drawn back, though the ferry was floating gently in the water. The service ramp was extended far below into the hull of the vessel and River could see the various cleaning and service crews busily entering and exiting the ferry. Boarding would begin soon. As he turned around he noticed a similarly dressed man standing up against a pillar. This one was different from the one before, but his mannerisms again belied innocence. He was reading something on a data pad, and looked to be speaking to someone through his embedded communicator. The man briefly looked up, met River's eyes and then turned by rolling his back round the pillar and walked away in the opposite direction.

I'm sure it's nothing, the commodore has me jumping at shadows. They can't be onto me already.

Twenty minutes later, the ramp extended and the boarding crew began the process. The ferry trip was going to be a full one. The boarding crew had opened up four gates and had extended six ramps to the ferry, to make the process quicker.

In hindsight I should have waited one night, and taken a ferry during the week when fewer people would be travelling. These look to be holidaymakers.

A short while later River was settled into his seat, with his satchel tucked behind his calves. The ferry shuddered as the engines engaged and lifted the hull out of the water. The continental ferry closely skimmed the ocean but did not actually sail the seas any more. It improved the speed, but in an emergency the ferries were fully seaworthy and could float and propel themselves along using traditional corkscrew water jets. Using lift-propulsion, the journey took two days versus a week or more.

The man who had been watching River walked past him on his way to the galley, looking briefly down at him. He returned from the galley shortly afterward with a bottle of distilled water and a glare from the stewardess. As he walked past him, he looked at River again and then up at the seat number.

River was beginning to feel highly anxious, but since there was nothing he could do he attempted to sleep as much as possible.

Two long days later the ferry arrived in New London. The continental ferry docks were in the same complex of buildings as the spacevators and so River was soon standing in a queue waiting to board the spacevator for the seven day journey off the planet. While on the ferry he had arranged tickets and check-in in advance, as well as a ticket to Ceres. Heading straight to the Jovian sector would be too difficult, considering that Jupiter and its moons were considered to be enemy territory. River's plan was to use old family acquaintances for the next challenge.

#

His eyes slowly fluttered open, the harsh light above causing the lids to fall down quickly again. He tried to lift his head, but it felt far heavier than it should and pressure on his forehead made it feel like his head was being held down. The left side of his body was throbbing and in the distance he could hear a steady hissing and beeping noise.

He hesitantly tried opening his eyes again and allowed for light adjustment; when the glare subsided he noticed that he was in a clinical room with various machines, the source of the hissing and beeping. He had been strapped down. He opened his mouth and, with vocal cords straining, managed to croak for attention.

Doors to the side of him swished open, and he heard

soft soled shoes patter up to him. The head that came into vision surprised him. It was the gaunt and pale face of a Hessr, human in feature but different enough to be noticeable. Hessr had larger, darker eyes almost bordering on black with large pupils and almost non-existent irises. Their noses were exceptionally flat with tiny nostrils, and most obviously they had small gills just behind their nostril bulges, which assisted with filtering out gases their bodies didn't need.

The changes in their genetics had begun happening roughly one thousand three hundred years ago, and then had begun accelerating dramatically during the last two hundred. Scientists believed that within another four hundred years the Hessr would look vastly different from humans, assisted by the magnetic radiation from Juniper's magnetosphere.

"Lie still, your body still hasn't healed properly." Hessr spoke the common language, although it was rumoured that they had their own language, similar to the ancient Mandarin.

"Where am I?" Stuart stammered, his vocal cords only slowly adjusting to the effort of speaking again.

"You are on Callisto, beyond the radiation of the Jupiter."

"My crew…"

"We can talk of that later. We recovered only you. You have been unconscious for almost six months. Please let me get the physician."

Before Stuart could respond the Hessr left. He assumed it was a she and that she was a nurse, simply by the human tendency for nurses to be female and by the fact that nurses only followed instructions set by doctors. The Hessr may be a differing species of the human genome but they were still very similar in their activities. Shortly afterward the physician did arrive, and he spoke little, mainly to ask for responses and pain levels from Stuart. He turned back to the nurse.

"He may be unstrapped, and we must begin physiotherapy on him as soon as possible." He turned back to Stuart. "You are a very lucky man to have survived. Your rehabilitation must begin immediately so that you can relearn to walk and build up muscle tone again. After six months, your body has practically wasted away. This won't be easy, and it will be painful, but you must persevere."

"What happened, doc?"

"Your ship came under fire and all on board managed to reach lifeboats. You must've been the last to eject. Shrapnel from the explosion of your ship struck your lifeboat and damaged its beacon and some of the life support systems. In response, the lifeboat put you into deep stasis. When we tried to revive you from stasis your mind did not want to wake and so we've been keeping you alive in the hope that your mind would return with time. And so it has."

"Why would you have fired on us?"

"We didn't." Stuart looked ready to speak again, so the doctor simply spoke over him. "Look, Stuart, I don't have all of the details. Our Chairs will want to speak with you when you are ready. Don't rush things. Only speak with them when you feel you are ready. I believe you will be hearing things you are not ready for just yet."

With that the doctor left, and the pain really started for Stuart. The nurses were rough with him and the physiotherapist even more so. Stuart would never have believed that one could forget how to walk in merely six months, but with his not eating properly his whole body had effectively shut down. The first meal was a chore to swallow, the first trip to the lavatories even worse. The first walk was impossible and he had to lean on the nurses for support frequently, even doing a wobble in the corridor at one stage. The physiotherapist had warned Stuart that he was learning to move again on Callisto and that his first trip to Earth would possibly be exceptionally challenging due to the much higher gravity on Earth.

Stuart persevered as requested, however, and in the space of a month he had regained most of this ability to fend for himself. He was back onto normal food and the pain medication was greatly reduced.

For the first two weeks of his rehabilitation the superiors the doctor had been referring to had left him alone and not requested to speak to him at all. Stuart had begun to wonder if they had forgotten about him. From the third week onwards the requests had begun to trickle in. By the end of the month he was being hassled for an audience almost hourly, and so he acceded eventually.

His agreement had seen him moved beyond his little medical world into a different part of the compound to what seemed to be more of an administrative section. There were a number of Hessr working at desks, behind screens, typing and tapping away at consoles. He was led into a small meeting room, where he sat for a few minutes before three Hessr entered. The doors swished closed and they seated themselves opposite to him. For a long while they just sat in silence. Stuart was not sure under what pretences he was being kept here, as a prisoner, as a hostage, or simply as a casualty of an attack. He was intent on waiting for them to make the first move.

"We are glad to see that you have recovered," began one of the Hessr.

"We were not certain you would," continued the other.

"We are hoping that we can come to an understanding," finished the last.

"Oh, I get it, you want repayment for nursing me back to health?"

"No, you misunderstand, Stuart," started the first again.

"What don't I understand?"

"Sadly, you don't understand much," answered the second.

"Hey, what's that supposed to mean?"

"We mean no offence, Stuart," said the third. "We wish to bring something to your attention and then we leave it up to you to decide how to proceed from there."

Stuart narrowed his eyes. This reminded him of those situations where someone was trying to sell him something over the communicator, making him feel guilty if he told the person on the other end that he wasn't interested. No obligation, always implied obligation to buy. "Continue," he simply said.

"Your Human Earth Confederacy is not what it seems, and it has been compromised," began the first. "But let me not be rude, and allow me to introduce ourselves first. I am Taliesin, this is Sepiesin and this is Dualiesin; we are three of the Thirteen."

"I'd introduce myself, but you already seem to know who I am."

"We know your name," said Sepiesin. "And your rank. But not who you are."

"Does that really matter?"

"No, it does not," answered Dualiesin. "What does matter is what we wish to explain to you."

Before Dualiesin had finished her sentence, Stuart had already looked over at Taliesin, expecting him to begin speaking again. He wasn't disappointed.

"The compromise to your Confederacy goes deeper into history; in fact the entire human social structure is compromised by an alien life form."

Stuart couldn't stifle the sardonic outburst of a

chuckle. "Next you'll be telling me the invasion is symbiotic."

"Well, no," answered Taliesin, breaking the pattern of one speaking sequentially after the other. He looked to his compatriots, confused. "The alien life form is parasitic, not symbiotic."

There was a moment of uncomfortable silence before Sepiesin continued. "The life form has throughout history invaded various influential people – leaders, politicians, warriors or generals, scientists and so on – for the purpose of spreading fear, terror and other agents of chaos and destruction."

"Do you have any idea how crazy that sounds?" interrupted Stuart again. "Why would you go through this elaborate exercise? You couldn't honestly believe I'd be so gullible to believe this?"

The three Hessr looked at each other not really knowing how to counter and to better explain themselves to Stuart.

"We can imagine that this is potentially a lot for you to process, but consider this, Stuart. Your race has had one dictator and warlord after the next, commissioning one conflict or one terror movement closely following the last throughout your history, since even before your historical records begun. Whereas we have not. For some reason, the Hessr are seemingly immune to this life form," reasoned Dualiesin.

"Then again, the Hessr genetic variation is much younger than ours, if I'm not mistaken."

"Ours is one thousand four hundred years old," stated Taliesin proudly.

"Not really that old to build up a history of real value, and in case you have forgotten, the Hessr are closely related to us humans."

"This may be true," retorted Taliesin out of sequence again. "However, other facts do stack up.

84

Such as all acts of aggression between Hessr and humans are only reportedly with our involvement. How much real substantiated truth have you come across?"

"Plenty can be backed! My whole family was vaporised by your kind." Stuart jumped up in anger. "I saw your ships in the sky firing barrage after barrage of energy cannon into my home town. I only escaped death by chance. I saw everything from the hill, coming back into town. Don't try to tell me you are innocent. I have had enough. Lock me up, kill me. Do. What. You. Have. To!"

"Please, Stuart," pleaded Sepiesin, but Stuart had already yanked open the door and left the room to march off down the hall ignoring the pleas.

He was fuming and his expression must have advertised that to all who cared to watch him sweep down the corridor. He walked aimlessly and no one made a move to detain him. He steamed for a while longer before realising that no one would detain him. He was free to move about as he wished. Without locking him up, they had still made him a prisoner. The HEC considered him dead and he was deep in enemy territory with no means to leave Callisto.

CHAPTER ELEVEN

The room was dark save for the bluish pinpricks from the *Online* lights from the nine displays on the far wall and the dim white light that shone down on the controls of the desk. The man seated behind the controls of the console was hidden behind the light. He was in his later years, shown by the stooped shoulders and the hairless head that occasionally reflected some of the white light.

His hands worked the console controls with confidence. The displays sprang into life, showing connection animations. One by one the screens brought a vector art of a meeting attendee, the individuals on the other side of the connection wished to remain anonymous.

A man's voice began the meeting, his was the top left display. The vector art highlighted in red as the man spoke.

"Sustenance production has decreased. Therefore we meet to discuss improving production. This meeting commences."

"I believe it is time for us to up the pressure on human civilisations," offered the bottom left screen, a female's voice, an older one, as was in evidence from the vocal cord strain and the rasp that only age added to a human voice.

"Pressure will not be sufficient, tensions must escalate to a new level," responded the centre screen, the voice of a male younger than the first with a strange dialect that was normally used on Mars.

"To what level are you suggesting, I wonder?" asked the man behind the controls. His was an older voice, measured and careful, a voice that spoke of intelligence and a habit of being heard and obeyed. All the voices carried the sense of power and control.

"To whatever level is necessary. As leaders it is our duty to ensure the Feeders create the right environments for the Breeders to consume and to breed," replied the middle screen, again with a slight sense of defensiveness.

"You have managed to not answer the question," chuckled the centre left screen with the sweet, innocent voice of a young girl.

"Bickering does not help further the objectives of this meeting," spat the top right screen with a patriarchal voice.

"I concur," added the abrupt and cold male voice from the centre right screen. "It is imperative we escalate the tensions and fear to manageable levels. Outright chaos, while producing the most ideal environments for sustenance, renders the environment unmanageable and the records of the eons clearly prove what happens then. Cleaners will be dispatched."

"These Hessr will become a problem soon, mark my words," stated the bottom right screen's mature female voice, ignoring the sentiments of the centre right screen.

"A terror attack should serve the purpose. If successful, it will cause the HEC to back down their war tensions in caution and shore up defences. The populace will most certainly become fearful since they would have expected the HEC to be protecting sectors regardless. Sector Defence Corps are underfunded due to the mobilisation of the Forward Corps," ventured the centre bottom screen with male Venusian tones.

The centre screen piped up. "Yes, I agree with that. A hard, quick and effective terror attack on a human installation that is critical to the HEC efforts."

"I don't think such a move is warranted, it's too brazen," interjected the centre right screen.

"How about Venus?" offered the centre screen.

"How about Mars?" offered the bottom centre screen.

"Stop your bickering, otherwise you will be ejected from this meeting," warned the top left screen.

"Earth?" suggested the bottom left screen.

"Ceres," stated the top centre screen in a flat tone. The almost bored male voice continued. "I will see to it immediately, Ceres is lowly populated but it will have an immediate impact on all human sectors at once, being the primary oil supplier for the HEC since the black gold dried up on Earth."

"All in favour?" asked the top left screen.

All screens voted yes.

"One last item that needs discussing. This Professor River Goldstein is becoming a nuisance. He has begun snooping where he shouldn't and needs to be eliminated. The episode with the agent was not enough to bring him to his senses and to keep out of the spotlight. This falls to you, number ten. See to it that he is silenced."

"I will do what needs to be done," answered the man seated at the controls.

"Personally? Surely not?" asked the centre left screen's fake innocent voice.

"No, I will use the agent again," answered the man.

"Good, then this meeting is adjourned," finished the top left screen.

All the screens winked out almost in unison leaving the room illuminated by only a soft white glow from the control desk. The man reached over to turn up the lights in the room and activated the communicator. It rang for a short while.

"Hello?"

"Hi, I have finished my conference. We have work to do."

"Yes, of course, where do you wanna talk, Professor Edison?"

CHAPTER TWELVE

Stuart's aimless wandering through the Hessr installation brought him full circle back to the corridor into which he'd burst earlier. He had concluded that the installation was indeed circular, similar to many of the human designed and built facilities.

What that meant to him, though, was that his objective of losing his three tormentors had failed and he had walked back to them. He entered the room and they sat in the same positions as they had previously. Patiently awaiting him.

Taliesin gestured to the chair he had vacated. "Please sit, Stuart, there really is no need for us to be getting off on the wrong foot."

Dualiesin continued for him. "You have been betrayed by your HEC. Sadly, we have little real proof, but we are sure that you secretly feel the same. There is no other reason. Why would they have a need to send you into the Jovian sector? The HEC is at war with the Ganymede Society of Life. They have not staged any operations in our sector for almost two decades. You were sent here to be destroyed. And we feel that this was orchestrated by these life forms."

"But to what end?" stammered Stuart, allowing for a moment to consider what these Hessr were telling him. "What would the Confederacy stand to gain by killing me? I am not important in the greater scheme of things."

"Exactly that, you are nothing to the Confederacy. You are not important and, therefore, you are expendable. It seems to us that the Confederacy is looking for a legitimate reason for escalating the war with us, since we are not moving to attack or harm our enemies. The Society is happy to have peace and wishes only to be left alone," answered Sepiesin.

"I need time to think. Where can I get a drink?"

The three looked at each other and turned their strange eyes back at him. Concern seemed to fill their only slightly human expressions.

"You will find the canteen in the extra-laboro section, any Hessr will direct you."

Stuart stood mutely and disappeared out of the door in search for something to take his mind off things.

#

The days ended up merging into one single grey blurred painting. Stuart's days comprised waking in a room, which he identified as being his designated cabin since he'd been cleared from medical treatment, then stumbling back to the canteen and consuming a basic meal to satisfy a gnawing hunger and then consuming the highly potent Hessr alcohol.

The transparent liquor reminded him very much of cane, without scent and with a powerful bite that took away one's breath with the first swig and one's senses with the second. How the locals were able digest the stuff without getting horrifically drunk was beyond him, but it served his purposes.

He was seated at a table, looking out at Jupiter and its striated surface and rings, none of the other large moons were visible today, but he wasn't at the table to gaze at the planet and its moons. He had considered for the millionth time what had led to his being on Callisto in the first place.

He was beyond the magnetic radiation of the planet and safe from apparent harm. It was a quiet way of life that the Hessr seemed to lead, lacking the bustle and the high energy pace that humans seemed to innately possess. It was a strange existence for him.

His eyes refocused as he noticed someone walk up to the glass. Focusing on the reflection he recognised Taliesin. This time the Chair was alone.

"Yes, Taliesin. I was wondering when one of you would want to talk to me again," he slurred.

"Stuart, I have come to have one last word with you. If you choose to drink yourself into oblivion that is your choice. But you will not do that here. Firstly, our alcohol is too strong for your weak metabolism. Ours is faster, as part of evolutionary adaptation to the magnetosphere. You will be sent away from us to live your life as you choose."

Stuart simply nodded, understanding that he had no place here and that they would want him gone if he was not going to be offering any assistance.

Taliesin continued. "We wish for you to travel back to your Confederacy and for you to engage with your leaders. We wish for you assist us in getting the message of peace across. We have sued for peace countless times before, but our communiqués have gone unanswered. You are a member of their rank structure, your returning from *death* will give you a chance to be heard. We wish for you to use that opportunity."

"And if I don't?"

"We will mobilise our android production."

"The android programme was abandoned and the creation of androids is a system capital offence!"

"To you, yes," sighed Taliesin. His shoulders slumped in sadness. "But not to us, we have merely seen ourselves the risks of intelligent mechanical life and have preferred to follow our own pursuits and quests of life fulfilment. However, this war cannot continue and we will have to retaliate soon. We are otherwise defenceless, our ships are not heavily armoured and we lack the numbers the Confederacy has at its disposal. You would leave us with no choice."

With that he stood.

"I will leave you to consider my words. Within the next week we will expect a final answer from you. Good day, Lieutenant Stuart Slate."

CHAPTER THIRTEEN

The people carrier had slowed to the speed required to navigate asteroids and the mood on board was tense. River had selected a seat near the front viewports to witness the last leg of the journey. Just below the passenger deck was the cockpit of the carrier, ahead of the cargo deck. The double decker was a fast and nimble vessel designed to ferry the few travellers that had a need for travelling to Ceres safely through the asteroid belt.

The pilots of these ferries were brave and highly skilled. Navigating the asteroid belt was one of the highest paying jobs a privateer pilot could be commissioned for, but even so, the list of willing pilots grew shorter and shorter. The large white orb of Ceres was just ahead, but numerous specks of asteroids still dotted the approach. Since its first visitor thousands of years before, the planet had managed to clear some of the asteroids along its orbital path which would eventually, some million years in the future perhaps, earn it a reclassification to a proper planet. For now, Ceres was still a dwarf planet and home to most of the asteroid miners' families.

The ruling family, the Queens, were long standing friends of the Goldsteins, and River was coming to look for their help. The Queens traced their lineage back to the famous Nigel Queen, the rogue asteroid privateer miner who had purchased his ship and been one of the first to mine the far-side regions of the asteroid belt. Far-side was a term most spacers used for a region that was on the opposite side of the sun to Earth, and therefore harder and taking longer to reach. Nigel had quickly attained wealth beyond compare, and had set up his descendants for lives of luxury.

In a moment, River would see Nigel's memorial.

The pilot manoeuvred the ferry in a steep downward tilt and brought her up suddenly to avoid two asteroids in a cross travel-path. He banked to miss a small, spiralling rock fragment and evened out the ferry, the sharp dips and twists unsettling an infant further in the back. River's fellow passenger, seated to his left, breathed out in relief as they entered the free zone around the dwarf planet.

The captain's voice crackled over the intercom. "Ladies and gentlemen, we have entered the free-zone. We will begin our landing sequence in the next two hours. We will be serving the final round of refreshments in a moment. Up ahead in the next ten minutes or so we will be passing the *Blue Queen* Memorial."

River had only been to Ceres twice in his life. In most cases the Queens had always come to Earth to visit his family, his father having decreed that the trip to Ceres was too dangerous. Eventually the trips had dried up as the kids had grown to adulthood and each had gone their own way. Of late, though, River had been thinking that since he was an only child he should re-establish contact with his old family acquaintances and keep the tradition going. It would be a pity if it all ended with him.

The *Blue Queen* was a real throw back to the initial days of space travel. A boxy aft design which contained an unpressurised cargo hold, tons of fuel cells and massive engines designed to thrust such an enormous vessel through atmosphere and vacuum, wings to achieve lift due to the absence of repulser technology in the days when she was in operation. The front contained all the functional decks, flight and control decks above crew living quarters, gyms, kitchen and other facilities needed. The ship's name and designation were on the wing tips with the crown logo of Queen Mining emblazoned on the neck of the vessel. In an emergency the neck would have been severed so that the fore-section of the *Blue Queen* could act as a lifeboat.

The *Blue Queen* had been encased in a glass cage and suspended in dynamic orbit around Ceres; she would always be greeting any visitor approaching the dwarf planet from Earth. She hung there suspended as a reminder of the origins of man's desire to conquer the solar system, the intrepid nature of his forefathers in space and the rising age of the spacer.

The ferry passed close by so that those on board would be able to catch a glimpse of history, but having a tight time schedule to keep to, it accelerated as soon as the *Blue Queen* passed by. The remaining time dragged on, but soon enough the stewardesses had begun cleaning and buckling things up. Passengers had all seated themselves.

The pilot began to slowly but steadily flatten out his approach vector the closer he got to the white orb, which soon enough dominated the forward viewports. Ceres was like most planets, other than Earth, mostly featureless unless one was a native of the planet. Its surface was all ice, all habitation on the planet was to be found in fissures that were abundant along the planet. Deep in the fissures life could survive with little scientific support, closer to the core the temperatures were warmer and radiation from the sun was tempered. The ice was also less dense and extracting water was easier. That far from the surface required artificial light, only midday allowed natural light to descend. But technology made the transitions almost unnoticeable.

Having gotten the approach vector right, they began to descend towards the surface and soon enough they were skimming along glaciers and peaks of ice. They flew over thousands upon thousands of fissures until in the distance the great canyon fissure of the capital came into view: Ceres Valley.

The ferry dipped into the white façade's crack, reducing its velocity and ever so slowly descending deeper and deeper towards the sub-surface city. The slick sides of the fissure seemed to sweat water the lower they descended. At level zero the sweat would turn into a cascade of water, which the inhabitants gathered and used for generating oxygen, among the more obvious uses, such as watering the plants in the many greenhouses in Ceres Valley, also known as CV to the locals.

They touched down without any incident and soon enough all the passengers were standing and stretching their lazy muscles. River hurried his disembarkation. He was anxious for his rendezvous.

#

The Queens had a substantial residence in the greener section of Ceres Valley. It overlooked the central gardens of the city, a large square space surrounded by silver, glistening spires. River was standing at the windows of the large sitting room overlooking the gardens and the southern cityscape. It gave him a sensation of tunnel vision due to the sheer white ice cliffs to either side of the city. Far enough away to not cause claustrophobia but always there, as a reminder of where one was. The furthest point, towards the south of the fissure or valley, was lost to sight due to the small size of the planet. Only four hundred and twenty kilometres in diameter, the natural curvature of the planet was easily noticeable, especially to visitors from larger planets.

River tore himself from the sight and went to make himself comfortable on one of the couches. His childhood friend sauntered in with his father in tow.

"River!" he called out in what River interpreted as fake excitement. The two of them had grown apart, that much was clear.

"Peter, how are you?" River stood and the two of them embraced briefly. "Nigel, good to see you."

Nigel Queen was a quiet man, studious and ruthless in business, though as soft as any when in the confines of his own home and his family. Nigel was the fiftieth of his name, in the long held tradition of passing on the name Nigel to the firstborn of the family since the first Nigel Queen had struck riches and started the family tree. The firstborn of the generation would inherit the leadership and absolute control of Queen Mining Corporation, the largest asteroid mining corporation in the solar system. Once Nigel decided to step down, it would be Peter's eldest sister, Nigella, who would gain control.

"I'm well," answered Peter. "Sit, sit. Can I offer you something? How 'bout a good whiskey from Earth? Something you're more accustomed to? Or are you up for some Ceres Valley vodka?"

"Just a single shot of whiskey if you don't mind," chuckled River as he sat down.

Nigel seated himself opposite to River, while Peter went over to the drinks trolley to see to the request. "Dad?"

"I'll have the same as River."

"Aw, you guys are no fun," mocked Peter. "I hear this brew of CVV is the strongest in centuries."

River choose to ignore the comment, instead he noticed the penetrating gaze that the senior Queen was casting his way.

"So what brings you out this far off your normal

beaten track?" asked Nigel.

"My missing friend."

"I doubt any of your missing friends would ever find their way here," laughed Peter from the trolley. He had just finished pouring the drinks and was heading over with two tumblers. River accepted his with murmured thanks. Nigel took his without evidenced gratitude.

"I need your assistance, actually."

"How can we help?" asked Nigel.

"I need to get onto one of your shipments to Ganymede."

"We don't have any shipments that go to Ganymede. To ship to Ganymede would be in contravention of the HEC sanctions against GSOL," replied Nigel.

"Nigel, I know that the Queens still send shipments of various ores to Ganymede. Your corporation is the only one wealthy enough to afford the jammers and technology needed to avoid detection by the HEC patrol ships."

Peter had seated himself next to his dad, and both of them were staring right through him. It had been a while since River had been in their presence, and while he hadn't forgotten about their mannerism, it was still unnerving to experience. Father and son both possessed an ability to stare right through someone while in thought. Their thought patterns and requirements took time for evaluation against risk and they would not allow themselves to be rushed into a decision. Once decisions were made, neither father nor son would ever back down.

"Right, we can get you aboard a shipment to Ganymede, but you will need to meet with the pilot yourself and without us present. We can never be implicated. These transactions normally happen through multiple layers of people. These are our shields. We cannot let that go to risk," committed Peter. His father simply nodded.

"I understand, Peter. Thank you to both of you."

"Why, may I ask, do you wish to travel to Ganymede? Is it to escape the trial?"

"What trial?"

"The rape trial," elaborated Peter. "I must admit, I would never have thought you had that in you."

"What rape trial? What in the name of the void are you talking about?"

"You mean you haven't seen or heard of the accusations? It's in all of the news, River," said Peter, completely incredulous.

"Peter, I think you should turn on the TV and play back the recorded news," suggested Nigel.

Peter snatched a remote off the coffee table and switched on the wall screen; he deftly switched the buttons around until he called up a recorded newsreel.

"*And onto tonight's headline story,*" intoned the lady on the screen. "*The father of the Galactic Highway project, Professor River Goldstein, is wanted for the rape of Doctor Shiori Wu. In a sworn statement, Doctor Shiori Wu explained the circumstances of the rape and cited fear for her career aboard RF601 as reasons for not speaking out about the crime sooner. The professor was last seen in Constantinople, where he managed to evade arrest and escape. The HEC is offering a reward of five thousand credits for any information that will lead to a successful arrest. Join us later, at nine, for the interview with Doctor Wu.*"

Peter killed the recording.

"I need you to believe me, I did not rape her. This is all a conspiracy theory. She's infected by an alien life form, a parasite that controls the actions of its host."

Nigel and Peter exchanged glances with each other.

"I'm not crazy!"

"Yes, River, it's OK, we believe you."

River could see by their pitying expressions that they didn't believe a word and most likely believed him to have gone insane. River realised then that they were only helping him because of their past.

"Either way, River," continued Peter. "Once you reach Ganymede, I suggest you don't come back to Ceres or contact us again. It's safer for us and, most importantly, it's safer for you."

River could only nod, and while it was saddening that his long-time family friends didn't believe him, he couldn't really blame them either. River was the first to admit that the story did sound far-fetched. People were also always inclined to believe the woman to be the innocent one, be it for something as simple as a case of infidelity or something as bad as rape.

"I suggest you lie low for the rest of the day, this piece of news will almost certainly be common knowledge by now and will have run in most bars or locales. The HEC guard will be on alert for you as well. It won't take science to figure out which transports or ferries you could have used to get off the planet. Tonight, when the city lights are dimmed, you can go to meet with our contact," suggested Nigel.

#

The meeting point was nothing like River's vaunted imagination could have prepared him for. He had fancied a smoky, dark, seedy tavern with raucous patrons and rougher waitresses, instead he found himself sitting opposite a clean-shaven and neat man in his early adult years at a high-class restaurant that used platinum cutlery.

"When the Queens arrange something, at least you

know you're in for a treat," chuckled the man.

"I see, of course," stammered River.

The waiter arrived with a bottle of red wine and a decanter. The smuggler went quiet while the waiter decanted the wine and set the decanter on the table and walked off. They had already ordered food. The smuggler poured himself a glass of wine, and made a show of inhaling the aroma. River stifled a sneer. The man was doing it all wrong, but he was the supplicant and so decided to rather be the meek one. This was his only hope of getting to Ganymede. Especially now that he had been accused of raping Shiori.

"Can we maybe get to business?" asked River.

The smuggler paused in his wine appreciation, casting River a surprised expression. He then relaxed his features, and inclined his head.

"But of course, to business then," he said mockingly. "So you wish to get smuggled to Ganymede?"

"Well, I suppose you could call it smuggling."

"It is what it is. Now you'll have to excuse me, but what do I get out of this run? This is, as you put it, business."

"I can't pay you much."

"Well, whatever it is you pay me, it must be more than five thousand credits," he barked out with laughter.

"Five thousand credits, I can't afford that!"

"I don't want five thousand credits, moron. If I was happy with five thousand credits, I'd turn you in. No, I want much more."

"You'd turn me in? Against the instructions of your paymasters?"

"Professor, you got it all wrong. I'm a freelancer. You're merely a contract. As is a shipment of ore to Ganymede. The deal is quite simple, they kit out my ship with tech, I do the run trying not to get caught. Sometimes I have to jettison the load if I get tractored or disabled for boarding. And when I finish, and the delivery is confirmed at point B, credits are transferred to me. I don't work for them, I do work for them. Big difference."

"Oh, well, then I guess I must find another way," said River dejectedly and rose to leave.

"Not so fast," the smuggler reached out and grabbed River's forearm, pulling him back down. "Sit for a bit, I'm sure we'll figure something out."

River sat reluctantly, not believing a resolution could be found. "Continue."

"I figure you wanna get out of HEC space quite badly, I also figure that you should be earning something out of your discovery even if you are not around. I did my homework, you patented your technology, which means you will get a royalty no matter what."

River nodded as he considered his words. While he wasn't wealthy now, in a few years he'd be richer than the Queens three times over.

"Here's my offer, I'll get you to Callisto. But in return I want you to pay me one per cent of all your earnings for the next five years. We got a deal?"

River thought it over for a moment. "Why not Ganymede?"

"I don't go that far in, too dangerous with the magnetic radiation and it's also the heart of their dominion. Callisto is dangerous enough."

"OK, we have a deal."

CHAPTER FOURTEEN

River was used to not luxuriating in upper class accommodations and benefits, but being stowed away in a lead shielded storage compartment with a hard pallet for a bed and just enough room to pace around in a circle for most of the conscious journey was a new low for him. Once the smuggler's vessel entered sub-light speeds he was put into a stasis chamber. The smuggler had explained that this run would have to happen by the old school method.

The GH was still off limits to the general public, though River had offered to rig his communications computer to send the correct signals to initiate a Passage. The smuggler had declined. He'd further commented that the HEC was monitoring traffic too closely, being highly suspicious of anything that got anywhere near the accelerator rings. And so they had faced a long four-month flight.

River, unlike most spacers, was not used to the after effects of stasis and so, post the hibernation, he was seated in the small passenger compartment just behind the bridge with a cold, damp cloth pressed to his forehead. River's scalp felt as if it were stretched too tightly over his skull and as if there were a whole colony of ants crawling around under his hair.

Jules, the freelancer-cum-smuggler on this contract, was just stepping into the passenger compartment. "We've made it into the Jovian sector exactly on schedule, and the fact that we're still around means that we weren't pulled out of sub-light by a HEC patrol. So that's good news. Callisto has just come into visual range."

"Great. So we will be landing soon?"

"Yes, there is just the matter of negotiating a landing. But our mutual friend should have arranged that already."

With that, Jules turned on his heel and made his way towards the bridge again. River decided he would follow into the bridge, albeit without invitation. *Considering what I'm paying for his services, I should have some liberties.*

His weak legs managed to support him in a stumbling gait towards the bridge when the whole ship suddenly rocked and shuddered violently. Jules' voice screamed into the communicator.

"Wait a minute! Cease fire! Cease fire!"

"Your codes conflict with the number of life forms we detect on board."

"The other life form is Professor River Goldstein. He is part of the shipment."

"Not according to the manifest we have. Your non-disclosure does not stand you in good stead."

"Please cease fire. I will deposit the other life form and extricate myself. I guarantee no attack."

"We will disable your ship and guide it to berthing by tractor beam."

River looked through the viewport and saw two Hessr ships, recognisable by the sweeping lines flying towards Jules' ship and peeling away out of sight as they blitzed past them.

"Hold on tight, a disabling shot tends to shake things up a little," he sighed. "Aside from the repairs I'll have to make. This job might just turn out to be a loss for me."

Shortly after his comment something hit hard, and true to prediction the ship rocked around even more violently than before. River was thrown off his feet and knocked his already tender head against the bulkhead of the portal into the bridge. Warning lights flashed and bathed the bridge in a red light.

"That's first. Now comes the disabling EMP."

That didn't cause any rocking, simply all the systems winked out and all the propulsion was lost. The gravity disappeared and River felt himself go weightless and lift into the air.

"Is all this necessary?" River asked.

"Are not so many things unnecessary?" harrumphed Jules. "This is going to cost a fortune to fix. I hope you're satisfied."

River chose not to rise to the bait. He started drifting back towards the passenger compartment. Jules pulled himself into his pilot's seat and strapped himself in. He called over his shoulder, "Strap yourself in, without gravity you'll be sticking to the back wall."

River reached out and pulled himself into a chair and buckled himself down. His headache had gotten much worse in the meanwhile and his whole body felt surreal as he lifted into the straps.

Being towed to the moon took longer than it would've taken them under their own propulsion. Time, however, wore on and soon enough they got to experience the rough and hard landing that was a result of simply being dropped to the surface by the towing craft before it powered away back into its patrol route. River heard Jules groaning in misery from the bridge.

He came slowly from the bridge and walked straight past River towards the exit ramp. He spoke without looking back, "You'll want to keep your hands in clear view." He cracked the glass cover over the emergency release for the exit doors, reached in and yanked on the release handle. With a loud hiss of pneumatic pressure being released, the ramp fell down. Almost within heartbeats a cadre of Hessr came racing up the ramp.

They rushed up towards River and before he could react he'd been spun around, forced to the floor and had his arms bound together behind his back. One of the Hessr confirmed River's status as being secured to what must have been his commanding officer.

"Why am I being treated like this?" asked River, his voice distorted from the force of having his cheek pushed up against the cold metal floor.

"Be quiet," hissed his Hessr captor.

River resigned himself to silence. He was hoisted easily to his feet, accompanied by a wave of headache-based nausea. He managed to swallow back the rising bile with great difficulty. He was guided roughly down the ramp and into what looked almost identical to the airlock that Stuart's *Benevolent* had landed in back on the Saucer. The large overhead airlock into space was closed now and he was guided towards the installation's entrance, where it seemed a prison guard was waiting for him. Jules was standing aside, a free man and not looking like he was going to get involved.

An officer, apparent by his differing uniform, stalked towards River and his guiding captors. As soon as he got within earshot, River started his argument.

"How can you simply arrest me and take me into custody? Without question or reason? This is against all etiquette."

"There is no etiquette in war, human, your Confederation decided that for us," sneered the officer.

"We share the same enemy, I am not your enemy. I come here in peace."

"Peace!" spat the officer. "Yet you conceal yourself by not disclosing your presence on board the passenger manifest transmission?"

"I am on the run from the HEC, we had to conceal my presence, otherwise I would be captured. Jules can vouch for me."

The officer looked over at Jules. "Is this true?"

"I'm not getting involved in this, sir. I want to

simply offload my ores and be on my way as soon as I can have my ship spaceworthy," answered Jules.

"Looks like you have no support there, but what did you expect from a freelancer?" chuckled the officer. "Now why would we want to harbour someone the HEC is after? The rule of shared enemies making likely partners is not the most supported in history."

"I have knowledge of the plot behind the war, and I need to find my friend who was shot down in the Jovian sector. I have reason to believe he was set up and is still alive. If he is still alive he would be in Hessr territory somewhere."

The officer hesitated a little. Usually quick off the mark, this was the first time River had managed to unbalance him.

"Seems a little ludicrous to me," he answered, unsure of himself. "Take him to a cell," he commanded the trooper standing to River's left side.

River was pushed forward and into the installation. He was being led down a long, slightly bending hallway, when he recognised a face.

"Stuart?"

Stuart was walking towards him, he looked drunk. At first he squinted in confusion, and then seemed to suddenly sober up.

"River? What in the void! Hey, you, what's the meaning of this? Why you got my friend in cuffs? Have you lost your mind?"

"Sorry sir, I have my orders, please stand aside," answered the guard to River's left calmly. The one to his right gently moved Stuart out of the way and they proceeded down the passage.

"River, hold tight. I'll get you out of this, I'll go and talk to their Chairs."

Stuart rushed off as fast as a drunken man could, leaving River to wonder what it meant to talk to a Hessr

Chair.

His little procession did not take long to bring him to a room, which was nothing like the prison cells River had seen as a guest at various HEC facilities. The Hessr seemingly did not fully understand the concept of incarceration. The room was afforded every luxury imaginable. The veneer of luxury only had a short term effect though, imprisonment still meant the chamber's walls were the limits of his freedom and soon enough the luxurious room chafed.

River was not sure for how long he was kept in the chamber, lacking natural light. There was no night time and since River had no concept of time he never dimmed or turned off the lights. River was also not in tune with Hessr or Callisto time and so the timepiece on the bookshelf made no usable sense to him. After what seemed an eternity, the doors slid open and two Hessr walked in.

"Our sincerest apologies for the manner in which you have been treated," began the one. "May I introduce myself. I am Quadiesin and this is a fellow member of the Chairs, Quiniesin."

River nodded, not knowing what was coming next. The friendliness might have just been a precursor with an aim to disarming him.

"Your friend Stuart Slate has made a strong recommendation for you, and insists you will able to assist him in exposing the threat of war by the paraci," continued Quiniesin.

That caught River's attention, it seemed like the light from the centre of the universe had finally shone some fortune on him. "By the Centre, you know of the paraci?"

Quiniesin seemed amused by River's sudden outburst. "We know of them, sadly we have no concrete proof as yet. But we believe it will be imminent. Our faith in the Centre is strong."

"So far, the Centre has given me nothing, but that's beside the point," said River cynically.

Both of the Hessr frowned at that statement, but they seemed to put it down to the lack of enlightenment of humans since they continued as if River hadn't spoken.

"Stuart is awaiting your presence. You two have much to discuss if you are to assist us in proving our innocence in this war," stated Quadiesin.

"We urge you to make haste," finished Quiniesin.

#

River quickly left the chambers and headed to where the two Hessr had said Stuart waited. Knowing Stuart, River assumed his friend to be highly impatient. Stuart could exhibit extreme patience, but only when he felt he was in control, such as when travelling at sub-light speeds across the solar system. In situations, however, where Stuart could do nothing but wait on others, the man was as impatient as a drunkard waiting for his booze.

As he stepped into the room, which sported an incredible view of the planet itself with Ganymede just rising off to its side, he was greeted loudly by his friend as he marched towards him with great intent.

"You, sir, are the last person I was expecting to see."

"When I heard you'd been shot down, I knew you weren't done for, so I came as quickly as I could."

"I've seen the news on you. River, tell me true, you didn't rape her? Did you?"

"You honestly believe I would do something like that?"

"No. No, I don't... I just... I just had to ask." Stuart

sounded embarrassed.

"It's OK, I understand that most people would take the woman's side before believing the man. How conclusive is the evidence?"

"From what was aired on the news? It's hardly conclusive, unless there is more they aren't showing... just some mumbled talk and a scream, that sounds as fake as it gets, on a recording. No video footage, no witnesses... hardly a strong case, I'd say," Stuart sounded convinced it was open and shut.

River dipped his head into his raised fist in thought. "No matter, that's not the priority for now. I heard you've been told about the alien life form?"

"Yes, the Hessr call it the paraci."

"What you think?"

"It seems unbelievable, but if it's true, it certainly explains a lot of stuff."

"That it does, and I have seen it for myself. I saw one burrow into Shiori. And I think they know I know. And that's why they are trying to discredit me."

"And that, that explains the rape charge! OK. So what now, Professor?" Stuart had a glint in his eye, like he was waiting for the challenge, and no matter what the challenge was going to be, he'd accept it.

"It's time we work out a plan to bring these paraci down!"

CHAPTER FIFTEEN

A green field stretched ahead of River, as far as his eye could see. Above him arched a perfect blue dome without a single cloud, the sun burning brilliantly in the midday sky. Not a wisp of wind disturbed his hair, not a stray scent offended his sense of smell. It was a perfect day. He began to stroll towards the horizon, not knowing what he would encounter. He was unafraid of what may come from the unknown distance. The peacefulness was suddenly interrupted as the sun began to flash with a red, intense light. A siren came drifting from just ahead, growing in persistence.

With a start, River sat up in his bed. A red warning light was flashing just above the door, and a steady siren was calling out. He stood up as quickly as he could and left his room, barefoot and dressed only in a light shirt and trainer slacks. A number of Hessr had left their rooms as well. Stuart was walking briskly towards him, fully dressed.

"The facility is under attack by the HEC, it seems. We've been asked to head to the escape pods, just in case the integrity of the facility is compromised," his friend said as he approached.

"Should we not be helping?"

"How? You're no fighter, River."

"I know that, but it's the least we can do."

"You're right, and I can fight, I have weapons training." Stuart was sounding committed. "Come, let's head there."

"Wait, let me get into my boots and clothes quickly."

River didn't need long to dress. He focused on getting his trousers and boots on and while trotting down the corridor with Stuart, he pulled his shirt on. Oddly, River noticed that Stuart wasn't rushing to get to the action. It was more a focused and measured pace, as if he were fully aware that the fighting wouldn't be over that quickly. They moved through the two sectors that had been abandoned by fleeing Hessr. Items and papers had been strewn everywhere in the commotion. Doors were slid into the open positions, not closing due to the sensor detecting obstacles. As they neared their destination they could hear the energy weapons firing away, followed closely by small explosions.

Stuart quickened his step to pass River, holding out his hand. "River, hold back, this might get dangerous."

River nodded; he respected and understood that he had little combat training aside from the basics he had been drilled with during his first few months in the Confederacy.

Stuart ran low to the ground almost in a crouch and quickly rounded out of sight. River slowed down to a crawl. His caution paid off – a red energy beam lanced out and struck against the ceiling, blasting the ceiling panel up and scorching the white enamel black. The sound was deafening. Although greatly surprised, River crept forward regardless.

As he came around the bend, he spotted Stuart crouching behind an overturned desk with two Hessr to his side, each armed with blaster-rifles. Stuart held only a light-blaster; he must've been given the sidearm by one of the Hessr. He was saying something to the one on his right. The Hessr popped up from behind their cover and began to pepper the far side with energy fire. As he started firing away, Stuart rolled to the side, then coming up in a full sprint he charged forward, dived to the floor and slid along the smooth surface to take cover behind a narrow but tall cabinet. His trailing wake was saturated with opposing blaster fire.

Stuart stuck only his blaster around the cabinet and opened fire. Shots were returned that buzzed alarmingly close to River, so he had to pull back his view. Small fires started up back down the corridor where the energy beams had finally struck against a surface. River ran back down the corridor in search of an extinguisher. The shooting exchange dampened a little as he ran down the corridor. He spotted an extinguisher, grabbed it off the hook and ran back up towards the fighting whilst removing the safety pin. River quickly put out the fire with the foam.

The shooting picked up in intensity, and suddenly ceased. Followed by a loud rumble that disappeared into the distance and then was gone. A few short blaster shots accompanied the rumble, but those sounded rather half-hearted.

River, still walking with the extinguisher in hand, approached the site of the fighting. Stuart was standing at a breach in the wall. The breach shimmered with the white haze of the magnetic shield that stopped the oxygen from rushing out into the void.

"It was an abduction mission," said Stuart as River joined him at the breach.

"Say again?"

"An abduction mission, the sole purpose of the attack was to abduct some Hessr and make off with some of their ships. Two came in, and four took off."

"What in the void for?"

"A set-up would be my guess," ventured Sepiesin, who had joined them without River noticing. "We will talk about it later, for now I wish to assist my brethren in putting out some of these fires."

"We'll help," offered River.

They set to work putting out fires and assisting the Hessr neaten things up as much as possible. The fires had begun to spread. Enamel took a while to burn, as did the exceptionally hard plastics that were manufactured for the structural components of the modern space stations, but once the material did ignite fire spread rapidly. It took them the better part of the remaining Jovian night to sort and settle the fires. By the time they were done they were exhausted, and Callisto was just making it around the apex of its night time journey and the sun was rising in the distance.

River and Stuart had just seated themselves on the floor near the breach, which was still being fixed up by Hessr wearing spacesuits and working outside in the vacuum. They needed to catch a breath. The Hessr could make do with much thinner mixtures of oxygen in the air than humans could and the strenuous work had left them short of air. The corridor was completely quiet, aside from the hum of the supply vents circulating wisps of air. The construction work happening just on the other side of the magnetic shield made no sound at all. In the void there was no sound.

They sat in silence for a long while, each lost to their own thoughts, when Stuart's sharper ear alerted him to something. He looked up.

"What is it?" asked River inquisitively.

"I hear people coming."

"Oh, well it was going to happen eventually. This is a public place," joked River. Stuart didn't seem to find it funny.

"Come, let's get up," he said and without waiting for an answer he began to stand. River sighed loudly, but stood anyway. Soon enough, the originators of the footsteps Stuart had heard appeared. It was the entire troop of Chairs, thirteen of the most senior Hessr at the facility comprising of six males, six females and a eunuch, who represented them at the next level up. The thirteen Hessr reached them in short order. They each wore an implacable expression.

"I am Uniesin," declared the one walking in the front of the triangular formation. "I represent both sides of the Seating, I am neutral to each side."

"That's nice," said Stuart cynically.

River shook his head. *He really can be rude.* The head of the Seating seemed to not hear it, since he went on in a monotone.

"We are all withdrawing deeper into our controlled territory. To Ganymede. You are welcome to join us, but it may be taxing for you to be so close to Jupiter. However, our shields will protect you for the short term. You are warned, though, you will have to leave within three months. Your frail bodies will not withstand more."

"We have nowhere else to go," said River, cutting Stuart off before he could make a mess of things. "We will come with you."

"Good," answered Dualiesin, who stood to Uniesin's left. "You have not reached a decision yet on whether you will help us, and we are loath to follow our alternative."

River looked to Stuart, slightly confused. His friend just shook his head and wore an expression that spoke volumes.

CHAPTER SIXTEEN

He deactivated the voice capture on the communicator, replayed the message and set it to repeat itself on the frequency his crew had agreed to use during emergencies.

"Benevolent *Captain seeks attention in the shadow of the god of gods. Sequence number 1*," repeated itself ten times, each time incrementing the number, before Stuart muted the speaker controls and locked the communication session against tampering. This had been the twentieth time he'd set up the recording, according to the intersystem protocol defined millennia ago. The protocol had never been reviewed due to its practical logic; the protocol for survivor emergency broadcasts demanded that the communicator software would deactivate the emergency broadcast after reaching a sequence number of eighty-six thousand. Messages could not be longer than eight seconds. This equated to roughly five Earth days before the message had to be recoded again. This ultimately meant that the message received would always be known as being fresh and needy.

Stuart pushed back from the console, and looked up at the screen that would display any reply messages. The communicator software that initiated the reply added a signature to the return message, which the original sender's software would be able to link up. The dashboard still read zero. Sighing, Stuart stood and grabbed his coat. His vision swam for a moment, and a piercing pain lanced through his temples. He only just managed to keep himself upright by gripping the backrest of the chair desperately.

"Not sure how much longer I can hold out here," he

said to the empty room. The symptoms of being so close to Jupiter were getting worse every day; his hair had begun to fall out during his morning ablutions. That morning he had pulled a fist full of hair off his head while washing, and he had undergone a small anxiety attack at that point. The DNA treatment was repairing him slower than the magnetosphere was damaging him. *Is this what the cancer victims of legend in the twentieth century went through?* he wondered, not for the first time.

The door to the comms-room opened while he was just recovering and in walked a Hessr, his expression painted with excitement. Which was to say, not much excitement betrayed the calm features; the amount he was showing was abnormal for a Hessr.

"Sir, please come quickly, something incredible is happening in Prison Block A," he practically shouted in a monotone voice.

"Prison Block? I didn't even know you had one, let alone enough to use letters to count them," Stuart managed to quip.

The Hessr looked at him confused. "We actually only have one, it simply has a letter in case we ever need to build more."

"Sarcasm really is lost on you people." Stuart shook his head, and before he found himself in yet another pointless debate about humour with another Hessr, he added, "Lead the way."

The destination was a fair distance away, and Stuart, who had only recently recovered from a long coma and was now hampered by magnetic radiation sickness, struggled to keep pace with the excited Hessr. He had to stop a number of times to catch his breath, staring up balefully through the transparisteel ceiling of the installation's top floor at the planet causing his discomfort.

Eventually they reached a long and narrow room. The room was an observation room, with one-way windows down both of its long sides. Through each window the Hessr would be able to look into two prison cells to observe captives. His friend was already there together with Taliesin and Quiniesin, two of the thirteen elders from Callisto, and three previously not seen Hessr wearing similar robes to those of the elders from Callisto, only with different colourations. Quite obviously elders from Ganymede then, since only Chairs wore robes fashioned in that style. River noted Stuart's arrival with only a flick of his head to gesture that he should come and look at what he was intently studying.

"What we got?" Stuart asked as he joined his friend.

"Just watch," River whispered distractedly.

Through the one-way glass Stuart witnessed humans twitching and convulsing on the floor of the cellblocks.

"They're dying, we gotta help them!" he shouted and made a move to leave the room. River grabbed his arm and pulled him back.

"No they're not, their bodies are ejecting something. You're not looking closely enough. These men are infected. The Hessr noticed their scarring between their shoulder blades when they took them captive, which is why they've been put under observation. Within a day of arriving, they've started to deteriorate."

"This is cruel, these men don't deserve this."

"Perhaps, but have we deserved what they have done to us, or yourselves?" answered Quiniesin. "This may be the single most important observation in the history of mankind."

"But... still, there must be a better way. What if you are wrong?"

"We are not wrong, Stuart," replied River. Stuart had never seen his friend so cold and detached. Was this his friend as the scientist? Or was he simply watching his revenge against this imaginary enemy? "The Hessr are largely immune to the magnetic radiation, we as humans are susceptible to the radiation, even under this heavy shielding of the installation. Their bodies," River was pointing into the prison cell, "are not experiencing any more harm than ours are at this moment."

"Look, look!" exclaimed Taliesin, completely dropping his austerity.

Everyone in attendance stared transfixed at the prisoner in the one cell. His back was arched, as he lay on his side. He was in a complete spasm, blood began to stream to the white enamel floor, as the scar began to split open on his back. He began writhing, and suddenly he rolled up tightly into a foetal position. With each convulsion, the captive gagged out lumps of brown mucous. The scar split open completely and slowly a wormlike life form began extracting itself out, backwards. The life monitors hanging above the observation windows flashed up at a second life form being present, then switched to an alarm indicating that one life form was busy dying and another was living. The monitoring systems were having a hard time deciding which was living and which wasn't.

Stuart spun around and looked to the other window. "It's happening there as well."

In the first cell, the life form had almost completely extracted itself. "From what I recall from the frozen life form I inspected, the head is arrow shaped and tapered to a point, it will have to tug hard to pull itself free," River said excitedly. He had stepped close to the glass and was completely absorbed. "I will want a closer examination."

The wormlike life form suddenly snapped free of its host and flopped, thrashing to the floor. It scurried around the cell, leaving bloody smears all over the pristine white enamel. It seemed to be searching frantically for a way out of the cell, when it suddenly launched itself into the air. When it landed it twitched once more and then lay still. All observers looked up at the life monitors, which read zero life forms.

In the other cell, the same scene had unfolded. The life monitors also read zero life forms.

"So much for the human bodies not dying, River," Stuart was angry and deeply disappointed in his friend. Revenge had clouded his humanity. Without waiting for a response, he stormed out of the observation room, his head feeling worse than ever, and his bowels cramping and ready for more diarrhoea.

#

Not many hours later, Stuart was standing in an entirely different observation room. This room was above an operating theatre. River was below with a few attendants dissecting the life form everyone had taken to calling the Parasite.

Quiniesin stood with him, it seemed that she had been assigned to him. She showed general ambivalence towards him. Stuart wasn't sure how he should feel about that. She had been talking again, and he realised that he had missed most of what she had explained to him.

"… So it seems that the Parasite has almost no tolerance for any kind of radiation. The human flesh offers very little shielding to them, perhaps enough for a single burst of magnetic radiation from a scan. But we suspect that even an X-ray is sufficient for them to be badly affected."

Stuart decided he should be paying more attention to what was being said; this discovery was a revelation.

Even though he didn't approve of the manner in which the discovery had been handled, it did offer information that was indispensable. If this parasitic life form was indeed the reason for all the major conflict and wars in human history, they might be on the doorstep of a long-term peace in the solar system.

"How is it that they lasted as long as they did here, if that is the case?" he asked.

"We increased the strength of the magnetic shields. That reverses and mostly softens the effects the magnetosphere had when we were brought on station. But we cannot cancel it out entirely. We haven't the power to do so. Even now, the shields are weakening daily. We cannot keep you here much longer; normally we run the shields at a tenth of what they are now. You would not survive here longer than two days, at most, at those levels," she explained to him. "We suspect that at those levels, this Parasite would die instantly, perhaps not even have a chance to escape its host."

"And it's impossible to remove these life forms and keep the host alive?"

"It would seem so. Professor River has already determined that when these Parasites attach themselves to the nervous cluster at the base of the skull and along the top of the spine they irreversibly damage the nervous system in the human body. It is through their life and mind alone that the host manages to continue living. It would also seem that they irreversibly destroy the host's mind. We must assume that they retain the host's memories, tapping into the stored memories in the brain. Which is how they manage to impersonate the host so well.

"Having access to the host's body means that the voice remains the same and only minor mannerisms change. It's a most beautiful deception, if that can be used as a description. Your friend is busy trying to determine what it is that nourishes their body. I have a gory theory, which I am not willing to share or test just yet."

Through the window, Stuart observed River speaking into a small recorder before he continued to scratch around on the Parasite. He then turned around and began to inspect the body of the former human host. The cadaver was lying on its front, the back and spine exposed. River was checking something below the skull, the gory remains obscured by River's shoulders and head.

"You must surely have a recording of this thing trying to pull out of the body of the host?" Stuart asked of Quiniesin.

"Yes, we do."

"We must get that on air, and show all of humankind."

"And get yourselves off this station, you also mean."

"That is an added bonus, yes. I grow weaker each day. I am retaining no food, and my headaches are wearing me down tremendously. I have no idea how River can concentrate like that."

"We feel your friend is driven by the emotions of betrayal and hurt. Adrenalin is a powerful pain suppressant."

"As soon as you can drag River away from that thing, we must be gone from here," Stuart said, the decision having taken hold in his mind. "Do you have a ship I can use?"

"Yes, we have a Confederacy ship you can use to fly back into your sector. Though it is mainly defenceless."

The doors to the observation room opened and a Hessr entered dressed in plain, unadorned overalls that most commoners wore. He bowed slightly and spoke in their native language; when he finished he left the room immediately.

"Your coded transmission has been answered, by a Jack Hayward."

"Jack! Jack is alive? That's great news. We must get going. Time to pull River back to reality and get this done."

CHAPTER SEVENTEEN

Nigel had been taking his leisurely stroll through the central park of Ceres Valley, as he had been doing for most of his life. It was his calming ritual. It allowed him focus and clarity of mind. It allowed him to reflect on the day's choices, and it allowed him to go home without the stresses that work brought bogging him down and affecting his family time. The day was yet another pleasant one, Ceres not suffering from thunderstorms or cloudy days as Earth did. There was minimal sunshine, only during midday. The bulk of the day was lit by the artificial lights mounted high up on the ice walls that were the perimeter of the rift valley in which the city was located.

The lighting systems were so cleverly programmed that they managed to mimic a rising sun, lighting a reddish haze that moved into orange and eventually the light of a normal day, then blended in with the midday sun and shifted over into afternoon sun.

Nigel had almost reached the most northern point of the diamond-shaped park. The wealthiest suburb of Ceres Valley was located here, higher than the rest of the city and overlooking the entire area. The Queen house was lower than the rest, but just across the road from the park. It was a position of standing and power. The seat of his family's control for millennia, passed down from firstborn to firstborn. A small smile of pride stole across his face.

The distinct sound of a capital ship's landing thrusters descended to Nigel, drawing his attention away from his destination and up the rift valley.

The rift walls darkened as at least fifty ships began to lower themselves down. Nigel recognised the GSOL logo, brilliantly emblazoned on the lower hull. Suddenly all the ships began to open up barrages of mass driver shots down towards the city.

The screams of the dying rolled from the city centre towards him, and he turned and ran towards his home with the same the panic as many of the other fleeing citizens did. Peter was running towards him, holding a mobile communicator out and recording the attack.

"Dad, dad! We need to send this to the Confederacy, they must send help."

"Peter, get downstairs into the bunker, quickly, before it's too late."

Nigel ran up and grabbed his son by his arm, turning him around and bolting as fast as his ageing legs could manage towards the mansion. His wife and youngest son were standing in the front doorway, staring transfixed at the scene unfolding in the city.

"Get into the bunker, now!" he shouted as he drew nearer. His wife and son seemed to come back to reality, as recognition dawned on their faces and they fled indoors. Peter ran past him, stirring up a brief wind. Nigel turned to look towards the city one last time, almost in farewell.

The GSOL ships were not big. They would hardly offer resistance to a big Confederacy warship, but they had caused substantial damage. Targeting the refinery first, the flames burned brightly. Soon the ice walls would begin to melt, and an avalanche and cave-in were inevitable. Ceres Valley may not ever be seen again. One of the capital ships, landing thrusters burning brightly, began to rotate. Nigel saw the barrel muzzle flashes and realised he'd lingered too long just before his vision went dark.

#

The commotion was deafening. The council was disturbed and angry. For fifteen years Jones had been leading and chairing the Confederacy Council and never had he needed to preside over such a decision. Not that the decision was a foregone conclusion, but by the body language of the assembling ministers he knew where this would lead.

The scribe was seated to his right, fingers poised over the keyboard. In a thousand years of judicial proceedings, never had a voice recorder been sufficient to record the law. Proceedings needed a human to record the situation to prove neutrality; a bizarre notion, but one that had stuck more for tradition than anything else. To his left was his aide, who would look up any contentious topics in the knowledge archives for a precedent or for reference.

As High Arbiter, the council would look to his final decision in the event of a voting bind. It was another bizarre concept that a council of uneven ministers could still be in a bind, but whenever contentious issues arose, inevitably someone would abstain from their vote thereby opening the doors to a potential bind.

It was another act that he had never been called upon to carry out. Even though there were abstainers, the vote always seemed to landslide one way or another. He had a feeling today would be the same.

He looked up to the doors in the distance. The council chambers were similar to an amphitheatre, a fan of rising embanked seats spread out in front of a pulpit from which a speaker would address the assembled ministers, behind which rose his desk with his scribe's and aide's desks to either side. It was a traditional set-up and had been around in one form or another for millennia as well. Humans, if anything, were a traditional lot, especially the politicians.

At what point did I become so cynical? he thought to

himself. *I think it may be time to retire.*

The doors had been sealed and most of the ministers were busy seating themselves. The High Arbiter of the Human Earth Confederacy stood, raised his judicial hammer and slammed it down on the wooden rest. A digital trigger within the smallish pedestal registered the knock and played out an amplified version through the speaker system in the chamber. The fifty-one ministers all fell silent, quickly settling themselves and looking up at him expectantly.

"Welcome on this grievous day to discuss an atrocious act," he began. "Less than eight hours ago, the Ganymede Society of Life betrayed the credo of their name and brutally attacked the Confederate City State of Ceres Valley. Thus far, we count no survivors and estimate total annihilation of all life. We meet to discuss our response and next course of action. I open the floor to the honourable ministers for discourse."

The Minister of Resources rose first, having tapped his button at his seat first. Each seat was equipped with a small keypad that allowed for votes to be registered, signals to be sent to his aide, or other basic communications. His aide would have received many of these signals and would arrange the order in which statements could be made. The Minister made his way to the pulpit.

"Fellow ministers, the act of violence alone is a crime against humanity, but let me put into context the importance of this event. Ceres is the centre for all mining activity within the asteroid belt. Most miners, not far-side, will return to Ceres to deposit their loads for processing and refinement. Ceres is the primary contributor of refined oil for the inner planets, accounting for well over seventy per cent. This attack leaves us short by some gigatonne of refined oil. This will affect practically all manufacturing in a negative way for at least a decade or more."

The minister finished without adieu or angry calls for action. He simply stated a fact that most in attendance would only have vaguely been aware of. The second opportunity to address the assembled fell to the Minister of Defence, as it was her zone of responsibility. The High Arbiter could see how this would turn.

The minister made her way down from the fan of chairs in a slow and measured step. She wore a general's uniform, not an admiral's, showing that she had made her way into politics from the Terran military troops. The arbiter knew that it often sowed a seed of resentment in the navy, who now made up the predominant percentage of armed forces. Stepping up onto the pulpit, she launched straight into her address.

"Fellow ministers, let me be brief. The act of terror and the complete disregard for human life can only be answered by one course of action. For too long, we have been idly sitting by while this strife has continued for decades. The Confederacy fields more troops, is better equipped and has a superior tactical advantage. I may be the Minister of Defence, but I have served in countless wars and I have held command in countless wars. Any general, admiral or other commander will tell you, offence is the best defence. And so I say, let us commit to all-out war and end this in one decisive battle."

She finished with some applause, but most ministers understood the gravity of the situation. High Arbiter Jones allowed more ministers the opportunity to speak, but all echoed the sentiments of the Minister of Defence. They went to the vote, and the results were counted. Jones spoke the words with a heavy heart.

"We will go to war with the Ganymede Society for Life."

CHAPTER EIGHTEEN

Stuart was highly excited. He had not expected any of his crew members to survive the destruction of the *Benevolent*, especially since he had been the only one to have been rescued by the Hessr. He barrelled into the communications chamber, flung himself into a chair and activated the communication controls, ignoring all the wooziness that exaggerated movements brought on. The radiation sickness was getting worse by the hour and he was anxious to get out of the magnetosphere and into normal harmless vacuum.

The reply message had come from a Confederacy deep space telescope that was aimed at the Gliese planetary system. It had been abandoned years ago. Stuart did not hesitate long before sending a poll signal out. It got answered almost immediately, meaning Jack had been waiting for the outreach. Stuart activated the voice communications.

"Captain Slate calling Lieutenant Hayward at Deep Space Scope 581D. Please come in."

"Cap, Hayward here, good to hear a friendly voice."

"Jack, you old coot, you're good and healthy?" The replies were taking a few minutes to transmit due to the distance, making the communication feel disjointed. Soon enough they settled into a rhythm.

"A bit beat up, sir, but living," Jack sounded relieved. "You coming to get me?"

"Yes, Jack, will be along as soon as possible. How are the life support systems?"

"Intact, though everything else has been gutted. I only have the barest of comms here. I have no locator sequencing displays, so don't know where you are."

"I'm some way off, but can get there quick enough.

What are the power levels there?"

"Running on solar only, most of the batteries are gone and only some of the carbon scrubbers are functional."

"How long you think you've got before you run thin?"

"If I'm clever with power and sleep a lot, I should be able to hold out some more weeks. Don't make me wait that long though." Jack forced a bit of a chuckle.

Stuart heard the worry clearly enough. He checked the readouts, confirming the distance. From Ganymede he was closer than any Confederacy pickup could manage, if he left now and if Jack had not managed to reach anyone yet.

"Have you heard from anyone else yet?" he asked of his crew member.

"No, not yet, but I have been sending out blind polls on the standard HEC rescue frequency. Been getting a little worried until now. Should've thought to use our frequency sooner."

"Don't worry about it Jack, I'm coming for you. Shut down your comms, I'll poll you when I get there with LOS. Keep all your power for life support, it's going to get rough soon enough."

"Roger that, Cap, see you soon. Over and out."

The communicator went silent. Stuart killed all the communication sessions and wiped the records. He then got moving. Before he had rushed to the comms-room he'd asked the Hessr to get the ship set up and ready for him, hoping that in the process they would have torn River away from his dissections and studies long enough that his friend could snap back to reality and realise that, as humans, they could not remain on Ganymede much longer. As it was, once they'd left the magnetosphere they would need cell and DNA repair while in stasis. The telescope was off the GH-route, which meant they would need to use stasis and sub-light travel to reach it.

Instead of heading for the science chambers, Stuart elected to head for the hangars and see if he could spot either River or one of their Hessr chaperones. He wasn't disappointed.

As he entered the hangar, not running but at a brisk walk, he saw the ship they were going to be taking. His friend was standing just ahead, appraising it. Stuart had to swallow a laugh – his friend would be appraising it not for the same features he would. River's appraisal would be entirely scientific, whereas Stuart would look at it through criteria such as styling and capabilities. The Hessr had somehow managed to lay their hands on some impressive technology. How they came to be appropriating this kind of ship was beyond him.

Only one ship was shaped like an arrowhead. Only one classification of ship was covered and layered with staggered panels of that sort of rubberised texture. This kind of vessel was incapable of atmospheric flight, lacking wings or propulsion systems that provided enough lift in high gravity environments. It could land and take off in an atmosphere, but that was it. As it was, the launch of this craft from even the low G of Ganymede would be assisted by a catapult system.

Parked in the hangar sat a stealth craft. Radar and other radio waves deflected off this craft's shape and skin in such a way that the radar pulse emitter would never notice that it had struck something. Its colouration was so clever that light practically bent around it. This craft's design and technology was the pride of the Confederacy, and somehow the Hessr had gotten their hands on it. The craft's classification name was Wraith, and it was well suited.

"How in the void did you get a hold of one of these?" he asked as he got within earshot of River and

Taliesin. "Actually, I don't wanna know."

"Captain Slate, have you managed to glean what you wished?" asked Taliesin.

"Glean?"

"Learn."

"Yes, I have. We must be off as soon as possible."

"I have given Professor Goldstein a copy of the security recordings that show the Parasite expulsion from the human bodies and we have copied the Professor's scientific findings into the databanks of the *Intangible*. When you reach your destination you will be able to upload the footage and the information for distribution to public news channels and broadcasting across the solar system."

"Great, get us hooked up to the catapult while we get ourselves strapped in and ready for our trip."

"Captain Slate, for your information, the *Intangible* has little in the way of weaponry. The vessel possesses only three turrets, each with a single light energy cannon, which will do little to a standard military energy shield and only minor damage to the average military armour plating. I would suggest you avoid a dogfight."

"I am aware of what the real use of a stealth craft is."

"That you would be, I guess. Also, for your information, we are not in possession of any torpedoes or space bombs. And as you will be aware, communication with a stealth craft is not possible by radio, due to its shape and composition. You will only be able to make contact by way of line of sight laser."

"No torpedoes will be a problem if we encounter capital ships, so we'll just have to be extra cautious. Unless we're burning high speed, no cap ship will scope us. River, let's go."

In the darkness of the void the *Intangible* slowed down to a halt and hung motionless, completely dwarfed by the gargantuan tube shape of the deep-space telescope 581D. River recalled the day the telescope had gone into service some thirty years ago. He had just gone into senior school, already on-track to becoming an astrophysicist, having been identified early on during his formative educational years as having the right acumen. It had been a major advancement in the search for extra-terrestrial intelligent life as it allowed for detailed surface analysis of planets beyond the solar system as much as four hundred light years away.

The telescope was as long as some moons were in diameter, the innards packed with mirrors and magnification lenses. The station was a minute little turret on the top of the tube, consisting of merely four levels. Living quarters, recreational quarters, storage, and the science level and a docking collar to the side. The scope could be adjusted by orientation jets that would vent carbon monoxide. A three sixty turn would take days to complete. The scope had been constructed in place, far away from other moons and planets to ensure their celestial light, no matter how insignificant, did not interfere with the magnified views.

The scope had been abandoned once life had been confirmed on Gliese and all scientific effort had gone to getting humans there. Now, forty years later, the first ships were only halfway there, and most likely would be overtaken by River's Galactic Highway's construction. To an extent, River felt sorry for those families that had decided to dedicate themselves to stasis and discovery. But such was the nature of discovery. It was not inconceivable that the scope might get used again to locate the next life-bearing planets. Understanding the habitable zones of nearby stars certainly shortlisted systems to look at. But with one confirmation, the Confederacy had a bone to chew on for a while.

The scope bore the name of the planet in the planetary system that was on the far edge of the habitable zone, and had been confirmed as bearing intelligent life. The evidence had been of constructed roads and gleaming buildings, as well as confirmed mechanical satellites orbiting the planet. The scope had done its job in an exemplary fashion. Humankind had discovered they were not alone, and that their nearest neighbours had their immediate space environment under control. Much more than that was mere supposition. The life could be hostile, but it could also be benign. It could be limited to their planetary system, but it could also be the bright centre.

Stuart was monitoring the station for any kind of signs of a trap.

"If it was a trap, it would be a fairly elaborate one to not have been sprung yet, Stuart," stated River, getting a little impatient.

Stuart remained silent for a long while, before he finally activated the line of sight laser communication.

"Scope 581D, this is the *Intangible*. Please come in."

His hail was greeted by silence, before the radio crackled and flared into voice.

"*Intangible*, this is Scope 581D. What took you so long?"

"I don't know what you mean. I'm here, aren't I?" Stuart laughed. "Meet us at the collar, I'm bringing the ship around."

"Got ya, come in steady, the collar got a little damaged when my pod hit it. But it's still operational and safe, just not that manoeuvrable. You'll have to come in nice and close."

"I'll be on the money."

River knew to be quiet and let Stuart concentrate. If the collar's computers were down, it wouldn't be a simple handshake and negotiation between the ship and the station. The ship would have to do the manoeuvring and the collar would have to try to meet up with the hatch manually. Stuart adopted a look of concentration as he flared up the light navigation jets and began the delicate steering to close in on the station, the various distance monitors feeding him with peripheral information his eyes and senses could not see or gauge.

If it weren't for the monitors, various lights and buzzers giving feedback, River would never have dreamed that the exercise was such a challenging one. In the vacuum of space, the ship felt pristine and peaceful with no rocking or shuddering. Simply a peaceful glide towards the telescope. In the viewports ahead, the telescope grew larger and larger until it eventually filled the entire viewport, with the detail becoming more and more apparent. River's attention drifted from Stuart's piloting and instead focused on the details of the tube.

The telescope was not a flawless tube of metal, but rather a sectioned tube pocked with hundreds of service hatches. All across the hull of the tube were loops that acted as ladders, and various anchor points for space-walkers to travel and work along the surface. As they got nearer, River began to feel the pull of the gravity well in the tube.

"He has his gravity activated, that will be drawing a lot of power. I guess the facility is in a better condition that we expected," declared Stuart, still focused on his piloting.

"I would imagine Confed wouldn't want to waste the investment. I'm sure a fair amount of maintenance crews still come out here and keep everything in check. More frequently now with the Highway being deployed everywhere."

"Uh-huh."

River fell silent, having briefly forgotten that Stuart was deep in concentration and would not relish his babbling. Having drifted into the gravity well of the scope the ship began to act a little more disturbed, gently shuddering and swaying as Stuart enticed the jets to push deeper towards the hull, while still using the mag-lifters to repel the ship away from the tube. It was a game of cat and mouse between artificial gravity and artificial anti-gravity.

"There it is, now to just…" In the forward viewports the docking collar suddenly drifted into view. Stuart began to flip a number of switches, the purpose of which River had no idea about.

"… Swing her about, and there," he finished punching some buttons and flipping switches in quick succession. The whirr that had been in the recesses of his attention disappeared. Stuart swung about in the pilot's seat, unfastened the restraints and headed back into the passenger compartment and towards the hatch. River belatedly followed.

By the time he'd reached the hatch, Stuart was glued with one eye against the small viewport that allowed the hatch operator a view of the docking collar. He was talking to himself.

"Just a little closer, Jack… there, there. Good."

He pulled away, looked at River, while yanking on the big release level. Down and then back up and back down again. The movement of the hatch lever had a double purpose, venting the pneumatic pressure that kept the hatch sealed and being a little more complex than a simple downward motion, which could be done by accident in the wrong circumstances.

"Welcome to Scope 581D," said Stuart swinging his arm toward the hatch in a mock welcome movement.

CHAPTER NINETEEN

River ducked through the low hatch of the stealth vessel and stepped gingerly into the docking column, feeling the colder air of the only just ventilated corridor. Switching between two vessels always made him nervous. He was fully aware of the dangers of space, and the statement he had overheard a moment ago regarding the damage from the escape pod still lingered in his mind.

He stood upright in the much bigger passage of the docking collar and waited for Stuart to step in with him. With his friend by his side, he walked towards the station.

Jack awaited them at the other end of the corridor, his arms crossed and legs apart in a foreboding impression of someone looking to bar passage. As they neared, icy cold blue eyes and a firm no-nonsense expression locked River's gaze.

"Who are you?" demanded Jack coldly.

"Jack, give it up," laughed Stuart, though Jack didn't break his gaze on River. "This is my childhood friend."

"Hi, I'm River," he greeted, extending his hand. Jack almost seemed to hesitate, then laughed and took River's hand briefly before warmly shaking Stuart's.

"Come in, come in. This damned collar will not be heating up and I'm freezing," he said as he turned to make his way into the station.

"We should not linger much longer here, the quicker we're gone from here the better," said Stuart.

Jack looked over his shoulder while he walked, but didn't say anything. His expression betrayed curiosity. "It won't take me long to power all the non-essential systems back down, so I can leave the station in the state that I found it in. We heading for Earth? Or back to Confed-HQ?"

"If you've heard from any of our other crew, I'd like to make a stop to collect them first."

"Stuart, we mustn't forget our primary objective," interjected River. That caught Jack's attention, and he raised an eyebrow in greater curiosity. Stuart on the other hand looked highly irritated by River's slip of the tongue, shaking his head.

"Primary objective, eh?" questioned Jack. "And what might that be?"

"We'll chat about that in due course, Lieutenant. Let's get wrapped up here and be on our way."

The rank-mentioning, change of topic line chilled the atmosphere even more so in the station as Jack wordlessly busied himself with packing up his belongings and powering down non-essential equipment, including the oxygen generating pumps.

"That's the last of the systems. Oxygen won't leak out, but it won't be replaced either. We have about an hour to get off the station, not that we need that long." Stuart picked up a torch, and switched it on as Jack killed the lights. River felt anxious without light.

"Uhm, Stuart, can I get a torch as well?"

Jack answered him. "You can grab one in that locker there. Captain, give us a hand with this chest here?"

"Sure."

The two military men grabbed a chest each, and began to make their way back to the *Intangible* with River in tow. Stuart headed straight for the bridge after depositing the chest he'd been carrying into the small cargo hold, while Jack busied himself with locking the hatch on the station's side of the docking collar. River moved to seat himself in the passenger's section, realising that Stuart would want his combat officer in the co-pilot's seat. While Jack was busy locking the *Intangible*'s hatch and releasing the grip on the docking collar, Stuart poked his head in from the bridge.

"We've got a Confed fighter coming out of sub-light at system's edge. Time to high-tail it out of here."

Jack didn't answer, but again he seemed confused by the statement. He simply nodded and went to join Stuart on the bridge.

The ship lurched suddenly, and River was pressed into his seat. Shorty afterward he felt the pull of the station's gravity release and the weak gravity of the ship kick in. After about thirty minutes Jack and Stuart came in from the bridge.

"Have a seat, Jack, it's time I filled you in on what's going on."

"I assume we've gotten away?" River asked rhetorically.

"Yeah, they came out of sub-light some distance off and their scanner would never have picked us up. So we made sure we tacked away from the station in such a way that the visual shield of the telescope would hide our engine glow. We're now far enough that we can accelerate our speed."

"That's a relief, Taliesin said this ship isn't a dogfighter." River almost bit his tongue off in shame of the second slip. Stuart didn't look pleased.

"That's a Hessr name!" shouted Jack. "You playing sides, Cap?"

"No, Jack. Relax. I'm not even going to try to explain. Rather, lemme play you something, and then I'll try and explain." Stuart went over to one of the monitors and tapped away, calling up the stored recording of the Ganymedian detention cell, Jack watching with widening eyes. After which Stuart and River explained, in alternating narration, the entire theory behind the Parasites and their objective. Jack attempted to throw various concepts around in a hope of successfully disputing the theory, but by now Stuart and River were thoroughly convinced of the theory and they managed to deflect all of the concepts.

"So what now?" asked Jack, incredulously.

"Well, we need to get to the primary Earth broadcasting satellite and broadcast this same footage together with a similar narration to what we've just given you. The narration will fall to River, since he has the scientific backing to make it sound less conspiratorial," stated Stuart simply.

"It's not that easy, Cap, and you know that. We'll need to somehow get past the entire fleet."

"We have stealth on our side, we can make it with some cautious flying. The trickiest bit will be taking the station without getting ourselves killed, and uploading the footage," said Stuart.

"What weapons do we have?" asked River.

"The ship has a light sidearm, and the Hessr gave me another light sidearm," answered Stuart, looking at Jack hopefully.

"Cap, that won't be enough. I scratched through the scope and found nothing. Confed had cleaned it out when they'd shut it down."

"So we have no decent way of taking the station?" moaned River, feeling very helpless and overwhelmed.

"Aside from weapons, three is not enough. And you have no real combat experience. Luckily, in answer to your question back at the 581D, I know where Dav is."

"Where?" asked Stuart quickly.

"When I sent out my barrage of emergency calls, Dav answered me. But he had been reassigned and couldn't come himself."

"Where is he?"

"He's on Phobos, the munitions depot on the

moon."

"That's very lucky," agreed Stuart, nodding vehemently. "We must push for Phobos then, before we go to the broadcasting satellite."

"Earth will be on the far side of the sun by the time we hit the Venusian sector. That will give us time to arm up and make the final run with some firepower," stated Jack.

"I noticed a light crawler in the cargo bay earlier," added Stuart. River just watched the two throw around ideas, each idea logical once voiced, but nothing that River would've been able to contribute to. Warfare, covert operations; these were all beyond his realm.

"There is one thing I do need to tell you, Cap."

"Yes, what is it?"

"This is a stealth vessel, so you've got no radio receiving capabilities."

"Not unless I angle the front deflectors up to open the shape."

"Fair, which you wouldn't have done. There was an A1 communication from Confed-HQ."

"A1? An imperative, all ships communication?"

"Yes. HEC has declared full-scale war with GSOL. All ships are to assemble at Luna Station, in preparation for an all-out assault on the Jovian sector."

"That is going to make flying to the Channel E1 broadcasting station almost impossible. There is no way we cannot be visually spotted with that many ships buzzing about. If we are flying stealth they'll be very suspicious of us. And if we're not in stealth, they will be able to scan us and demand we communicate with them," reasoned River, essentially stating what everyone was thinking.

"We'll think of something between now and hitting Phobos. No point letting this mountain overshadow us now, without us being anywhere near it," said Stuart.

River recognised when Stuart was trying hard to be optimistic. The last time he'd heard that tone was when he'd left the Saucer for Ganymede.

"I'm more worried that it will take us too long to get to the broadcasting station," said Jack. "Surely the point of this all is to get this out before all-out war begins?"

"Agreed, but we have no other way," Stuart was beginning to sound deflated.

"I have an idea," ventured River hesitantly.

"Let's hear it," asked Jack.

"We can use the GH."

"Too dangerous," stated Stuart firmly.

"No wait, hear me out. We can fly through one ring, drop out, take stock and bounce forward by another ring. It's not as fast as just hitting each ring until our destination but it's at least ten times faster than convention sub-light travel."

"If we pop out of a ring, we might pop right into a very sticky situation."

"Yes, true, but I know the codes to the GH. I can tell if something is using our entrance ring as a destination. We can skip around them or get the warping to bend us around them, or we can wait for them to pass. It's a whole stack of queries I'll have to run, but it's nothing major. I can do it, perhaps script it and repeat them at each ring as the scenarios broaden through our experience."

"Sounds like a risky experiment, we can't take the risk" shrugged Jack, looking at Stuart for approval.

"Yes, we can't take the risk. Let's move out. Phobos, here we come."

Part 3

Map of Jovian System, 3050-10

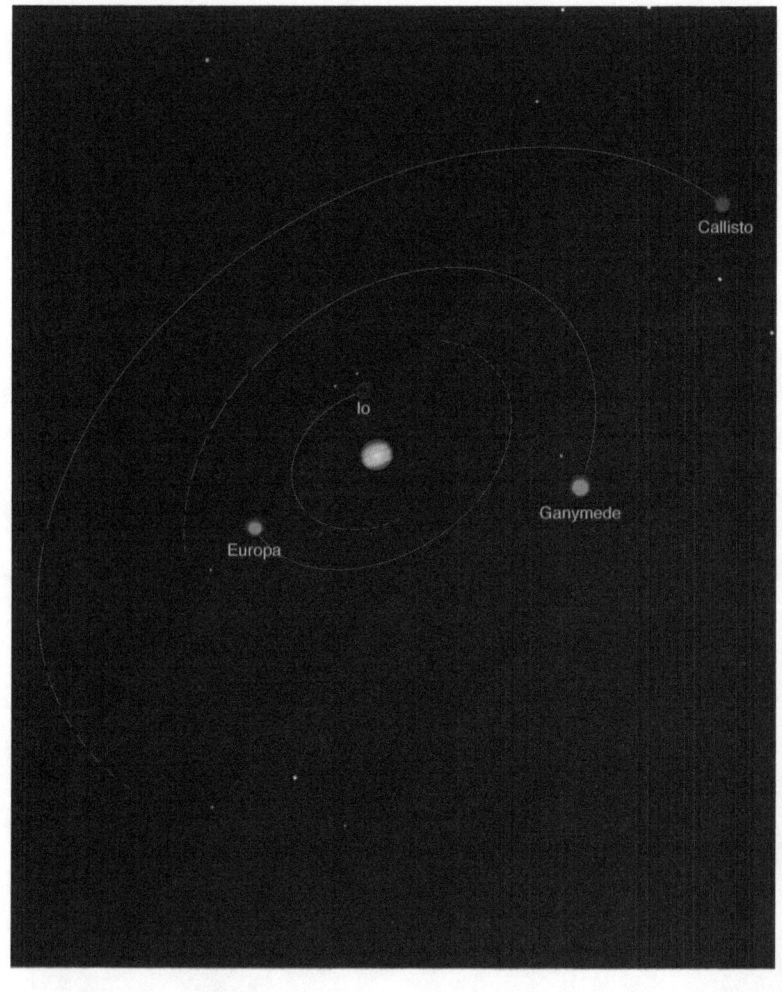

CHAPTER TWENTY-ONE

The *Intangible* had just skimmed past Deimos and was slowly catching Phobos as the little moon raced around its planet, Mars. Stuart had piloted them in such a way that they had yet to be detected, but he had to be careful to avoid notice. They were in a stealth vessel, true, but that didn't stop them from being spotted visually. Though the odds were poor.

In the vastness of the void, there were many routes to follow that would have avoided contact, but few pilots would travel routes that were not direct. Flying in circuitous routes could let one get horribly lost, and in most cases it was prudent to aim directly for a reflective source and use these bodies of reflected light as waypoints. Which was exactly why they had aimed for Deimos when they had left the deep space telescope.

Stuart piloted the vessel to bring it up behind Phobos, rather than flying directly towards the moon. That put the bulging side of the moon on the far side. Phobos, unlike most other celestial bodies, was not round. This had to do with its size; it was so small for a moon that it didn't spin itself into an orb. Slowly it was growing in the viewports as they neared.

"The weapons depot is on the far side. I'll put us down on the surface and then let us drive towards the rising sun, the drive should take us less than an hour. The moon is only eighteen kilometres in diameter. I just want us to stay in the blind spot to avoid notice," explained Stuart.

"Good thinking, Cap," answered Jack confidently.

"We doing a space walk?" asked River hesitantly. He hadn't been in vacuum in only a suit for a few years, and even when he'd been in frequent practice at it he'd always been nervous. The suits were precariously thin and he constantly had flashbacks to the training videos that warned against floating space debris tearing the fabric and causing near-instantaneous death.

"We're not walking, but, yes, near enough right," came Jack's sarcastic reply. "You could sit this out, I suppose."

"No one is sitting anything out, we'll need all hands," cut in Stuart, before River could reply. "Jack, have you gotten the message off to Dav yet?"

"No, Cap, I will need to get closer so that we don't need line of sight. And obviously you'll need to drop the stealth mode so we can get a reply."

"Not chancing it to simply get a reply, we'll send the message, touch down, travel to the ground entrance and hope Dav is ready for us. There is too much risk any other way. You two get suited up, and ready my suit. As soon as we've touched down, I want us out on the surface."

Stuart had spoken, and River had no urge to argue with his friend. In this Stuart had more experience firstly, and secondly also held rank over Jack and himself. Jack also remained quiet and went over to the communications console and waited for Stuart's signal to send the encoded message over the low-band frequency radio waves.

Jack received his signal as soon as Phobos completely filled the forward viewports and began to swell into the overhead viewports. The moon might have been among the smallest in the solar system, but she was still eighteen kilometres in diameter and up close eighteen kilometres was a substantial object. Thereafter Jack and River got themselves suited up.

Stuart slowed the *Intangible* even more and began to

level the ship out to begin a landing approach vector and within a short amount of time he had extended the landing gear. Extending the landing gear disrupted the stealth shape and made the ship detectable by radar. It was all part of the risk.

As soon as they touched down, Stuart released his seat restraints and jumped into action. "Let's get moving people, we're detectable now and it won't be long before someone notices that a vessel has landed on the moon."

In darkness of the Phobian night, they rushed towards the back and helped Stuart into his suit, opened the crawler hatch at the back of *Intangible* before popping the personnel hatch and extending the ramp onto the pitted and cratered surface. Cautiously they left the gravity of the *Intangible* and stepped out into the much lower gravity of Phobos. They had strapped weights to their suits to decrease their buoyancy, yet they still bounced to the moon-crawler, which awaited them at the top of a short ramp. Soon they were rolling over the harsh Phobian surface, heading towards where the sun would be rising in two hours.

The weapons depot soon appeared on the horizon just as River was beginning to get agitated with the ride. The moon-crawler was relatively large with a substantial loading bay on the rear, designed to move rock ores and other discoveries from source to waiting space craft. Not normally stored in stealth ship cargo holds, the vehicle would have to be left behind once they had offloaded the weapons and munitions. The depot was a flat building and not tall, it hugged the side of the raised lip of the Stickney Crater. The depot descended a number of levels down into the core of the moon. Its design was to minimise any impact damage from any strikes that got through the asteroid defences. There was only one surface entrance. The usual way into the depot was by landing directly into the depot's airlocks. It wasn't a large weapons depot, but it did get its fair amount of traffic.

The sun had not fully risen yet, and was still hanging mostly below the horizon. As they got nearer, Stuart switched off the moon-crawler's spotlights and began navigating in the dim light of dawn.

"How will we know if Dav is ready for us?" asked River into his headset.

"Shhh, radio silence," crackled Stuart's reply.

River felt his face heat up in embarrassment. Jack brought the moon-crawler to a halt behind a small mound of rock. The two military men climbed off and, using small bounces, they inched their way to peak around the mound at the facility. River sat watching them in the dim light for what felt like an eternity. He felt decidedly useless. Stuart waved him to follow and the two of them began long bounces towards the depot. As River rounded the mound in a hurry to catch up with his companions, he saw a single light flashing rapidly in their direction a few times before being extinguished.

They covered the distance quickly, making sure that their bouncing didn't raise them too far above the surface and beyond the grip of the moon's gravity.

A man in a vacuum suit awaited them. Once the airlock had closed and pressurised, the man removed his helmet. The moustached face smiled broadly. Jack and Stuart had removed their helmet at the same time and were already clasping hands in welcome. Though not talking to each other, it was evident that the three of them knew each other well. River did not need to guess that this man was Dav Sensler.

Dav motioned for the three of them to follow and they set off after him, while River struggled to remove his helmet. His companions were intent on their business and didn't stop to help him. River didn't want the help. He knew what they were about. Dav led them down a myriad of empty corridors.

"This is the quietest time in the station, I had to work some serious miracles to get the graveyard shift," he whispered, as he pushed in a security code to open the doors to the weapon cache. The door swung inwards silently. "My code is authorised into this room, but we won't have long. I have authorisation, but without any orders to be here, someone might notice and wonder why I've come in here. We must hurry."

Jack and Stuart both nodded, and rushed in. River followed urgently.

"River, get a maglev trolley. Jack, you grab the rifles. I'll get the energy packs and chargers. We can charge on the *Intangible*," ordered Stuart.

"Cap!" Jack grabbed two charged rifles and handed one to Stuart, who slung it by its strap over his shoulder.

River took a sidearm for himself, knowing that a rifle in his hands would serve no benefit and may be a danger to his companions. He had little idea how to use a weapon effectively, having only received basic sidearm training after he'd joined the Confederation before taking up his position on the Saucer.

"River, stop messing around, where is that trolley?" River blushed again, and rushed off to fetch the maglev trolley.

Jack and Stuart had already selected the weapons and munitions they wanted and as soon as he arrived they began to load up the trolley. Dav poked his head into the cache.

"Hurry. We're nearing the wakeup call," he whispered in an urgent tone.

Jack added a tripod to the trolley and, together with Stuart's assistance, they lifted a heavy anti-personnel cannon to the trolley.

"We're done here, let's get going," said Stuart, sounding like calm incarnate. River's pulse was racing, and it felt to him as if all in the room should be hearing his heartbeat knock against his rib cage.

Dav took point with Jack and Stuart walking to either side of River as he guided the trolley back the way they'd come. Dav headed out well ahead of them, in the eventuality of intercepting someone. Jack had brandished his rifle, while Stuart had decided to draw his own sidearm, probably deciding that he didn't want to decimate the depot in the event that energy fire was exchanged.

They quickly reached the hatch, and while slipping on their helmets the alarm went off.

"We got to move, Dav, hit the emergency hatch release, we don't have to time wait for pressure equalisation!" shouted Stuart.

Dav hit the button, and the four of them hurriedly fitted their helmets. With a loud whoosh the air rushed out of the hatch that blew open. The rushing air tugged at them. River didn't wait for any signals and all but flew the maglev trolley out onto the barren Phobian surface.

As they bounded across the rocky moon surface, River looked over his shoulder and spotted gunners taking position in the defence turrets of the depot. The barrels swung around and took aim. Energy fire erupted in spray around them. River panicked but managed to keep the trolley going.

Jack and Stuart opened fire back at the station, even though their rifles and sidearms would have no effect on the tough armour plating of the depot. Stuart peeled away from the path that River was following hoping to draw fire. Jack did the same in the opposite direction. Dav followed River's path and had now drawn his sidearm, shooting blindly over his shoulder back at the station.

A thick green beam of energy struck the surface just ahead of River, showering rocks everywhere and kicking up a plume of grey dust and debris. River dived to the ground, letting the trolley glide forward. He felt the debris striking his back like hail in a storm back on Earth. His fear of a suit tear threw his sanity with the same ferocity as the stones in the instructional video. A strong pull lifted him to his feet. Dav had pulled him up and was urging him onwards. Somehow River managed to make his body function and he bounded forward and regained control of the trolley.

More energy fire fell around him and he tunnelled his focus on the moon-crawler. Stuart and Jack had already reached it and his friend had already started it up. Jack's voice came crackling over the headset. "Hurry, hurry. We gotta get going!"

River shoved the trolley towards Jack, who stepped aside, took control and began to quickly unpack the trolley's contents into the crawler's loading bay.

River climbed onto the back seat of the crawler and looked over at Dav, who was still pointlessly shooting back at the depot.

"Dav, get back here, you're not... Dav! No!" Stuart screamed as green energy fire pulverised through Dav, vapourising him with energy levels designed to push through capital ship armour. Jack's scream joined in with Stuart's. River went numb.

"Cap, we gotta go! Cap!"

Stuart snapped out of his blank stare at the place where Dav had stood. His friend looked at the loading bay of the crawler, confirming that everything had been loaded. He engaged the vehicle and began to race back towards the *Intangible*.

"They will be launching fighters to intercept us, we have little time," said Jack.

Stuart didn't answer. River guessed his friend was well aware of the process the depot would follow. It was surprising at what speed they had been able to man the turrets, getting the pilots up and into the fighters would take longer. Normally a larger attack would give a greater amount of notice. The pilots would be scrambling.

They reached the *Intangible* without any further attack, having lost the depot beyond the horizon and now being effectively out of visible range. Jack and Stuart busied themselves with loading the cargo bay up with the stolen weapons and munitions, while Stuart went to the bridge to start up the engines. As Jack slapped the hatch's closing button, the Ripper-class interceptors skimmed over the horizon, closing quickly.

"Go, go, go!" shouted Jack over the headset. River needed no encouragement. He had just stepped on the ramp, when he felt the *Intangible* lift off the surface. He had to grab a handhold to stop himself from falling back to the moon's surface. With a struggle he pulled himself into the airlock and closed the hatch. The airlock pressurised quickly.

They stepped into the main hold of the *Intangible* as Stuart shouted new orders from the bridge. "Get to the turrets, and hold them off if necessary. These are light fighters, we can lose them if we make a run for it. They can't stray too far from the moon."

River had no idea how to use a gun turret, but he ran for the nearest one. The *Intangible* had three turrets, top, bottom and rear. Jack ran for the rear turret, River took the top. He just hoped that the light fighters would not try to exploit their underside. River had just strapped himself into the gunner's seat when the *Intangible* rocked heavily.

The radio in the turret squawked. "They're in range and are firing on us. Hold tight. Initiating evasive manoeuvres. By the void! Return fire!"

"On it, Cap," came Jack's answer.

River was petrified, he had no idea how to use a turret's weapon systems. From the corner of his eye he could see through the turret's transparisteel viewports that Jack was returning fire. The hypramium stealth panels rotated around to expose the titanium armour plates. He focused on his controls, looking over the various buttons and levers. A series of consecutive explosions caused Stuart to come back online and scream for him to return fire as well. He located the activation switch, slapped it and roared in victory as the turret barrels extended from their idle cavities. He gripped the control sticks and swung the barrels around in search of a target.

He quickly found one, but before he could pull the trigger the *Intangible* banked away in an evasive turn. The interceptor's energy fire harmlessly flew just above his turret.

Lucky there, I was almost sheared right off the Intangible, he thought to himself.

River corrected his aim to compensate for the new flying angle, and pulled the trigger. Half expecting some kind of recoil and not experiencing any left him a little surprised but he showered the general direction of the interceptor with dangerous energy. He completely missed, but he did make the interceptor shy away. The *Intangible* banked again, heavily. River swung his turret to face the back of their ship, getting a view of the trailing fire that Jack was laying down. One of the interceptors was taking a high line behind them and was within River's and Jack's sight. Both turrets opened fire, catching the little interceptor in a cross fire of green energy wash.

The fighter couldn't withstand the barrage and exploded.

"Yes! We got him!" shouted River in happiness. His mirth died down quickly though. These pilots were actually on his side.

"Boys, the other fighter is disengaging, we've put enough range between ourselves and the moon."

River deactivated the turret and relaxed a bit in the gunner's seat before returning to the bridge. Jack was way ahead of him, and River only caught the trailing part of the conversation.

"…we'll have to stop somewhere," Stuart was saying.

"What's up?" asked River.

"We took some serious hits in that little dogfight, nothing threatening, but enough to damage some of our stealth capabilities and our docking collar," answered Jack.

"I was focused on evasive manoeuvres and rotated our armour plating after we'd already taken some hits. Straight after take-off the particle shields are still weak and they got some shots in," explained Stuart.

"That's it then, our mission's over," sighed River.

"Stop being so melodramatic," snapped Stuart, uncharacteristically.

"Sorry," frowned River.

"We're a long way off from Earth still, and Venus is closer. We can find cover in the underground movements there, get some repairs before Earth comes around the sun again. We have some time. Not much, but we have some time," explained Jack.

"The trick will be flying without stealth. We will have some more dogfights coming our way, for sure," added Stuart. "The time on Venus will also give us a chance to plan our job at the satellite and try to not make the same mistakes we made at Phobos. River, Jack, get some rest. I'll fly us for a while, before I can get us to a vector where it's safe to use sub-light engines again. This was the first strike, we have some more to go."

CHAPTER TWENTY-TWO

Venus was today what Earth should have been a thousand years ago. Tranquil, temperate and full of modern technological marvels that most humans back on Earth had yet to experience. The planet was roughly the same size as Earth with a twenty hour day. Five hundred years ago, terraformists had accelerated Venus' rotation, stopping it just short of the twenty four hour mark when costs ran too high. The increase in rotation had been enough, however, and life had slowly begun on the once desolate planet.

Terrans had all tried to vacate Earth as quickly as possible, until the administrators of the new colony had put a stop to it, citing that one of the reasons for Earth's descent into anarchy and turmoil had been overpopulation and the inability of the natural cycles to reasonably sustain life. The new Venusian ecosystem was at that stage still too fragile, even more so than Earth's. And so they had put a quota limit on new arrivals.

Venus had, since that decision, remained a close-knit society with little immigrant traffic over the centuries. The population had expanded slowly via highly controlled breeding programmes on-planet. Women and men were not allowed coupling. Family planning was a complicated matter, requiring authorisation by the governing bodies after a marriage had been proven stable after a minimum of five years. Populations on other planets had, at first, through movements, demonstrations and petitions, attempted to provide free choice to Venusians but it quickly turned out that they liked it that way.

Ironically, Venusians had not become prudes. In sexual revolutionary terms, they were enlightened and frequently engaged in various public sexual encounters that would be considered taboo on many other planets. Having careful family planning and stable marriages meant that acts of sex were encouraged, especially since love on Venus was considered transcendent of emotions such as jealousy and insecurity.

This meant that ironically, aside from rare fresh produce and other goods not seen on Earth in hundreds of years, one of the major exports from Venus was the sex trade, with sex-workers travelling all over the solar system plying their trade. Travelling sex-workers meant spaceships, and spaceships meant shipyards. It was towards one of these that Stuart was busy piloting the *Intangible*, under guidance of Jack, who was a descendant of Venusian grandparents. His parents had been the rare kind that left the planet for good, never looking back and finding it more pleasant to settle on Earth herself.

That did not mean that Jack didn't embrace many of the Venusian ideals. One of the primary reasons why he had never married and settled down with kids, remaining in Confed active duty instead, was that Jack had struggled to find a partner as sexually *enlightened* as he was.

The *Intangible* entered the atmosphere and began the descent towards Olympus, the biggest city on Venus. The spaceship shuddered and rattled heavily as they flew through the high winds, which buffeted the upper layers of the relatively new atmosphere. Venus's terraforming had only been finished two hundred years ago. The planet was now the second blue orb in the depth of darkness, making her title as Earth's sister planet even more apt.

Olympus was a picturesque and perfectly planned city that covered most of an island, green and verdant, surrounded by crystalline waters that teemed with aquatic life. The closer they got, the calmer the heavy winds became until eventually the detail of the city became more visible. The architects and planners of Olympus had drawn beneficially on centuries of lessons learned by their Earth counterparts. As such the city was perfectly laid out, in concentric patterns that spoke of logic and thought. At the high altitudes only seven streets could be identified. These streets were actually highways, and they formed a symbol known through human civilisation. The symbol was of two concentric circles interlinked. The symbol was lost the closer they drew to the surface.

"Please make your way to berthing V101BH. Uploading clearance codes now," said the air traffic controller's female voice over the communicator.

"Confirmed, thank you," answered Stuart before muting the communication channels again. He glanced at the scanner, which was busy updating grey crosses with appropriate friend or foe colour overlays. Their berthing was highlighted by a larger yellow cross. Stuart flipped a few switches and the scanner's black featureless background changed to a real-time terrain image. "We'll be touching down in a few, I suggest you guys strap yourself in. We're now in a gravity environment."

"Personally, I can't wait for some natural air to breathe," chuckled River.

"Venus can hardly be called natural," said Jack as he laid a hand on River's shoulder before turning around and heading into the passenger compartment. "After all, Venus is a terraformed planet. She's man-made."

They touched down with little fuss, and while Stuart was busy powering down the various systems, River opened the main hatch and extended the ramp down. He was anxious to breathe air again. Even though Jack insisted the air wasn't natural, it was certainly subjected to natural forces now that the terraforming was complete. Venus had gained its own atmosphere and had been maintaining that man-made atmosphere with no artificial influence for almost three hundred years now.

River stepped down into the berthing, which was essentially a metal circular platform of roughly sixty metres in diameter; it was a berthing meant for light ships. From various concealed hatches rose support and maintenance facilities to resupply or drain various tanks of refuse or fuel. Venusians were walking towards the *Intangible* from the terminal buildings. Surrounding the terminal building were numerous other berths and platforms. In the spaces not occupied by functional buildings or structures, the Olympian architects had planted large sentinel trees to provide some greenery and beauty.

Stuart strode past him, intercepting one of the Olympian officials. They began sorting through the various berthing permits, while Jack led River in addressing the offloading of their personal belongings.

"I suggest we find suitable lodgings for ourselves, not too far from where we can arrange repairs and not too far from here so that we can leave as quickly as possible should the need arise," offered Jack.

"I would agree with that," said River.

They began packing the crates containing their weapons onto a maglev trolley, not unlike the one they had used on Phobos. By the time they had finished Stuart had joined them. They walked in silence towards the terminal buildings, where they hailed a transporter. Across the road was the larger freight terminal where a number of enormous freight ships were coming in for berthing. Other major exports from Venus were the perfectly shaped, highly organic vegetable and fruit exports. Venus, being in such a perfect natural equilibrium, grew the best foods. They were expensive and in high demand. The farmers of Venus did not over produce and only exported once a year.

Once they had loaded the transporter, and seated themselves in the back seats behind the driver, they realised that they had not really agreed on a way forward.

"So where to now?" quizzed River.

"Jack? This is your neck of the woods," chuckled Stuart.

Jack was silent for a while before he answered. "Driver, please take us north on the Eastern-Male Bypass, to the second Em Octagonal, Barley Street Inn."

Stuart and River, never having been in Olympus or even on Venus said nothing and quietly sat back to watch the scenery pass them by as they joined the main highway and began looping in what would have been the northerly direction Jack had requested. For the first part, the view from the left of the transporter was only the spaceport. It was a vast complex of terminals and berthings that seemed to dominate the landscape. Not in an obscene manner; the architects had quite successfully managed to integrate a multitude of little streams and rivulets between the sentinel trees and the glass and steel structures of the spaceport itself. It was a grand scene to see a spaceship lift up from amongst the trees and then blast off towards the Venusian heavens. They left the spaceport behind after the highway took them underneath another highway that curved off towards the south. The left view was then replaced with cityscapes, alternating between commercial skyscrapers, and parks with residential homes or apartments back to commercial landscapes. The view out of the right-hand side of the transport showed nature with fields and orchards that were only just identifiable in the far flung distance.

From the highway the city looked prosperous and clean. River was sure though that as with all cities the underbelly would be rank and full of scum. What Olympus did better than any other city he had visited during his time was draw a veil over that hidden life.

An hour later the transporter pulled to a stop outside a humble looking double storey house in a suburb with wide walkways, white picket fences and big front gardens. Each house was styled according to the idyllic 1960s American family home. It was a throwback to the history lessons that were given about the life of the first space travellers. Although the spacers of the time, astronauts were supposedly an elite few taking years of training and preparation before embarking into the void. It was a concept that River struggled to come to terms with. In 3050 travelling to the void was like travelling to the shops for some milk. It was simply a matter of choice.

The driver unloaded their baggage from the trunk, depositing the bags and chests on the walkway. After receiving his payment via the portable biometric credit machine he left in a hurry.

"Shall we get ourselves inside?" asked Jack.

"What is this place?" asked River.

"This, my friends, is the home of my second cousin Jennifer. It has been some years since I visited here. But one will always find a place to rest one's head if in town, and she will always provide nourishment and refreshment."

"Lead the way," suggested Stuart.

The three of them, each taking as many bags as he could lift, managed to load up the bulk of the baggage and trundled up the long footpath to the front door. Before they could reach the steps that led up to the porch, the front door opened of its own accord and a young looking woman stepped out from the house. She was exceptionally good-looking, blonde and with a ready smile. She bounced from the entrance of the house towards Jack.

"Jack! By the Centre, it's been ages."

"Jennifer, you're looking good too." They embraced warmly as only family would that had not seen each other in ages, whilst one of the pair was heavily encumbered.

Jack pulled away as best he could. "Jenn, this stuff is heavy, can we get inside?"

"Of course, of course. You can drop your things just on the left in the lounge. No one uses that."

She led the way into the house, showing them the direction while heading towards the back of the house. They carefully stacked their load, before Jack led them to the back and into a large kitchen that looked like something from the history videos. The stove was styled to look like the gas stoves used in the twentieth century, now illegal due to the contribution any kind of gas made to greenhouse effects. The Venusians would be especially sensitive to those concepts. River suspected most of the appliances in the kitchen were merely for show, since the packaging of the products now performed most kitchen functions.

Jennifer had set out tall glasses and a big jug of lemon juice with ice floating on top, yet another throwback to the history lessons. She must have noticed River's expression of surprise and bewilderment.

"Yes, this is lemon juice. Unlike Earth, Venus has the ability to naturally produce goods that Earth once could some thousand years ago. Living up in the void or on Earth, you would not be able to find real lemons. Though some do find their way to Earth. Only a handful of people can afford luxuries like that," she chuckled.

River felt his face flushing. "I can imagine it would be an expensive import, flying a couple of lemons to Earth. There are more important items that need to be shipped long distances. Hopefully the GH can fix that."

"GH?" Jennifer looked slightly confused.

"The Galactic Highway," clarified Jack. "This here is Professor River Goldstein, the inventor of the GH."

"And on the most wanted list," finished Jennifer. "I've seen the news footage. Though I must say, you don't look the type."

"The type?" asked River.

"The type to be able to rape a woman. I've experienced a few of those in my time."

River was too polite to ask her to clarify, but he suspected by that statement that she must have had some bad experiences in her past. If she took to the same traits as Jack, River suspected that Jennifer also possessed a bit of wanderlust.

"I am innocent, that I can assure you. This is an elaborate plot and we're on a mission," explained River.

Jennifer started laughing. "My, my. You sound just like someone from the movies. All heroic. So cute."

River felt his face flushing again.

"Jenn, let up. He's talking the truth. By the Centre, I wish it were not the case. But we're wrapped up in something big."

Jennifer stopped laughing and instead seemed to consider the three of them. Stuart, who had been quiet up until now, finally spoke up.

"Look ma'am, we certainly don't want to inconvenience you. We just need a place to lay low for a bit, while we have some repairs to our ship completed. Then we will be on our way. We simply want to stay out of sight, and out of mind for a little bit.

Jack brought us here saying that you'd help. But we also understand that you might not want to be associated with a wanted fugitive."

"Oh, I don't mind providing you with a shelter. Just don't go bringing my business into disrepute. Jack, what you need?"

"I need to get back to the berthing and oversee some repair work," Jack answered her. "The captain can fill you in." He turned to Stuart, "Sir. I will proceed back to the *Intangible* with your permission and get started on arranging contractors to start the repair work."

"Yes, Jack. Do that. Be careful with payments, credit transactions could be traced back to your location."

"Shit."

"What?" asked River.

"I paid that transporter by biometric credit."

"That means we have roughly four days before they're onto us," stated Stuart. "We won't be able to stay here."

"If that. Cap, you'll have to oversee repairs. I know this city better than either of you, and must now look for other accommodation."

"No, Jack, you don't know it better. I do. Let me take care of that," offered Jennifer.

"No, ma'am, you must not get implicated or involved in any way," said Stuart. "I will go to the berthing and arrange repairs. Jack, you find accommodation."

"And what about me?" asked River.

"Sorry, Riv, you stay here. You'll get in the way, and you're the prime witness and subject matter expert on the Parasites. You must be protected. Exposing you to anything is not an option."

"Oh." River felt useless all over again.

"There is the matter of credit tracing; how will we

pay for anything?" asked Jack.

"I'll have to figure it out," said Stuart. "Maybe barter something."

"I have some cash," offered Jennifer again. "It's not much, but perhaps you can use it as a deposit to get work started?"

"Jenn, no," objected Jack.

"It's OK, Jack, you can pay me back when you can."

#

Parts supply had delayed their repairs by a week. Now after six days of lying low in rented apartments on the southern-side of Olympus, as far away as possible from Jennifer's house in the north, the three were ready to move all their belongings back to the new berthing. Aside from having moved themselves to a different location, they had moved the *Intangible* as well, recognising that should the authorities trace their movements to Jennifer, they would be able to find the ship and possibly impound it, effectively ending their mission.

On the third day, Stuart had returned to the apartment and had informed them that he had caught the news that the entire fleet was assembling at the Luna Space Station and that in roughly one month's time they would be leaving to attack GSOL. Time was running out. Especially since they needed to still travel from Venus towards Earth and cover many millions of kilometres.

Stuart and River had gotten all their belongings ready to be transported back to the ship and now just awaited Jack. This time around instead of arranging a pickup, Jack had borrowed a vehicle from his cousin's business. It was an unbranded delivery transporter with privacy panels across the loading area. Perfect for their agenda.

"I still think we will have to chance using the GH," stated River, for what must have been the hundredth time. The three of them had repeated the argument on many occasions, Stuart and Jack oscillating on opinions either in support of River's suggestion or against. "It's the quickest way to Earth, and it reduces the risk of us arriving too late."

"The GH is Confed patrolled and controlled. How do you expect us to travel it undetected?"

"I have a theory."

"You keep saying that, how 'bout you share your theory and then we can see if it will work."

"I am hesitant to share my theory."

"Why? It's not like there is any harm."

"OK, fine. I designed and built the anchor rings. And I built the traffic system as well. We can handshake with one anchor ring and query inbound traffic. The traffic system will be able to inform me whether there are ships inbound and what ships are in the proximity of the destination ring. Each ring is equipped with a fully up-to-date FF scanner so that it knows which ships are friendly, and which are foes. It was a requirement of Confed that the rings not activate themselves to enemies of Confed."

"OK, that's great. But we are enemies of Confed. Surely HQ has gone and blocked us then from using the GH?"

"Yes, I imagine by now they must have."

"OK, so there goes your theory."

"All developers leave backdoors."

"What you saying?"

"I'm saying that I have a way into the system. A backdoor. One that Confed doesn't know about."

"How sure are you that Confed didn't stick their

own engineers on it and found it?"

"Not a hundred per cent, but sure enough. Confed has too much on the go to worry about that. And even if they did, I hardcoded my backdoor into each ring and each ring is a slave to the next. And each ring backs itself up to the next. The sequence to override the coding is very difficult. I designed it like that on purpose so that one ring couldn't compromise the next."

"That's brilliant!"

"If you say so." River was never good at handling compliments, but while he felt awkward at the compliment he did feel happier knowing that he could contribute to the cause.

The front door to the apartment opened up and Jack slipped in. "We've got to get a move on, I think Confed has traced our ship. There is a swarm of activity in the military section of the spaceport. I noticed it while driving out."

They rushed the packing of the loaned transporter, not bothering to secure any of the cases or bags. If they got stopped by the Red Guard and checked they would be fined and held up, but they had to get moving. Luckily, speeding was not possible on city highways due to the controlled magnetic tracks that guided all driving vehicles in an accident free pattern.

The terminal to their berthing was busy with various cargo transporters delivering crates to outbound cargo ships. People were hurrying in a coordinated frenzy. River and his companions blended right in. The berthing was empty save for one of the port officials who had to sign off the clearance papers. Stuart had arranged their departure a day ago and simply had to digitally sign.

"What about the vehicle? Don't we need to take it back?" asked River.

"No, Jenn said she'd send someone for it in a day's time," answered Jack.

Stuart was already on the bridge warming up the tertiary systems; once those were warm and online the sequence for the secondary systems could start. Pilots would usually shut down all the systems when ships had been idle for longer than a week and thereby save equipment from wear and tear. Pilots who expected to be underway again in under a week would normally leave the tertiary systems idle. With tertiary systems on standby, launch procedures were much faster – mere minutes compared with almost an hour.

"Guess it's goodbye Venus," said River, wistfully turning from the cargo hatch to head for the passenger ramp.

"Halt!" came a shout from the entrance doors into the terminal. A cadre of Red Guards came rushing towards them. Three knelt down and levelled barrels at them. River threw his hands up in the air. Jack came around the back of the *Intangible* his hands raised as well.

"No use bolting. The ship isn't warm enough to go, they'd take us down before we could even blink."

CHAPTER TWENTY-THREE

River had been detained in a bare, concrete room that was in stark contrast to the otherwise colourful and beautiful world of Venus. The room had no windows; only a luminescent ceiling that provided a glaringly bright white light. In each corner was a boldly displayed camera, superfluous since two cameras would easily be able to record any movement in the room. In the centre of the room was a square chrome topped table with a centre leg and with a single aluminium chair at each side.

It was not meant to be comfortable; it was meant to make the arrested feel uncomfortable and anxious about what was to come.

He had been seated facing the single door into the room for some time now, having been separated from Jack and Stuart during the arrest. He was unsure of where his companions had been taken. He'd managed to form some kind of friendship with Jack, though he was mainly concerned about his friend.

I'm fairly certain that they'll not charge Stuart for anything, it's me they're after, he considered, not for the first time. *Unless of course they know what happened on Phobos? But surely that couldn't have been immediately linked to us, none saw us or managed to get a reading on the* Intangible *during our flight?* And so his thoughts went in spirals.

River was renowned for his over-thinking and the incarceration with no outside stimulus released his vivid imagination to a full flight of fancy. He imagined a lifetime of wrongful imprisonment in a deep-space penitentiary. He imagined gang-fights and rape. He imagined being forgotten by the world and even forgetting who he was.

He was suddenly shaken from his dark thoughts when the door opened to admit a uniformed security officer and a man dressed in a fancy, well-tailored suit.

The man placed his briefcase on the table, pulled out the chair opposite River and sat down, not saying a word while he opened the briefcase and pulled out a digital filer. He activated the filer and flipped through some readouts.

"Your list of HEC bylaw infringements is short but severe, Professor Goldstein. HEC has been looking for you for some time, and you have been skilfully evading arrest. But your days were always going to be short-lived. None can hide forever," he started.

"I've not been hiding, I've been about gathering evidence to prove my innocence," replied River more confidently than he felt. His hands were clammy, a sure sign of his nervousness, but he kept those steady, palms down on his legs under the table.

"I'm sure you were," chuckled the suited man. "Let me cut to the chase, I am a Federation Attorney. I will be the prosecutor during the trial, I have a long list of evidence that to me proves you are as guilty as sin and have a heart as dark as anti-matter."

"I haven't been given a chance to elect a defence attorney," objected River. "And last time I checked, I'm entitled to that."

"That you are."

"And furthermore, I also shouldn't be speaking to you without having consulted with my attorney."

The Federation Attorney nodded. "So I will take it then that you will not talk to me openly. I was hoping that you would see reason and we could avoid going into a lengthy court case, when you are so obviously guilty of the rape. The Federation is keen on making an example out of you, and is not afraid for this to go to court or to cause a bit of publicity. I was simply hoping we could avoid that, for your own sake."

"For me, of course." It was River's turn to be sarcastic. River had seen this kind of personality before, it was an almost exact replica of his former superior's megalomaniac personality. The FA was seeing an opportunity from which he could improve his reputation and find some kind of glory through prosecuting a high profile case.

"You are being charged for first degree rape, obstruction of justice and contempt of court by the Supreme Court of New London."

River gasped. Confed certainly was looking to make an example out of him. He took a while to compose himself; the FA was taking pleasure in River's discomfort.

"I would like to speak with my friend Captain Slate. Is he under arrest as well?" he said, subdued.

"Captain Slate has been excused for siding with you. The HEC determined that his incident with the *Benevolent* near Jupiter was reason enough for his lack of judgement and his lengthy seclusion in Hessr territory was reason enough for his unawareness of your crimes."

"So does that mean I'm free to speak with him?"

"You are. I will send for him. You will only get ten minutes of privacy with him."

River nodded his understanding, deciding to say no more. The attorney packed his filer into his briefcase, stood and left the room. The security officer followed him out, leaving River alone to his thoughts and his fears.

#

River had struggled to keep his impatience under

control, and had eventually stood up and begun pacing around the small interrogation room, much to his own chagrin. He would never have believed the anxiousness that had overcome him with his detainment. His freedom snatched away.

Incredible to believe that I was located in one deep-space facility for so many years, effectively trapped, and I'd never felt this feeling then, he considered. *I guess I could have left whenever I wanted to.*

His wait must have been long, because a warm meal was brought in and consumed, albeit without discernment of flavour, before Stuart was let in. The guard who had opened the door briefly looked around the room from the doorway suspiciously.

"What you looking for? Suspect I might have engineered my escape with this plastic spoon?" snapped River, unable to hold back his frustration.

"I see they have managed to break down your patience?" asked Stuart, looking highly concerned.

"I'm very frustrated, Stuey."

"I can imagine. They have been treating you well, though?"

"I suppose they have. I've been fed, but haven't seen anything aside from this table and these chairs since being brought here."

"No one come and spoken with you? Surely someone?"

"Oh, there was someone. A Federation Attorney. He was very rude."

"All prosecutors are rude, that's what they're supposed to be."

"I guess so," answered River dejectedly, as he pulled out his chair and slumped onto the cold aluminium seat. "Where have you been?"

"Jack and I got pulled up in front of the CO of Venusian Confed. He's a Brigadier, quite high up in the ranks. He declared us as unwitting accomplices and that due to my disconnection from reality after the attack and my lengthy time as a hostage on Callisto, I could not have known what I was getting myself involved in."

"And? You let them buy that?"

"Well, it's true."

"But…" River was about to launch into an angry tirade at Stuart's apparent throwing in of the towel, when it struck him that his friend was simply putting up a show. Stuart wore a slight smirk, one so slight that most people might have missed it. River had grown up around him and so knew the signs. *The rooms are under surveillance, they are listening in on us talk. Hoping I give something away.*

"Anyways, River, you must admit to your guilt, and hopefully it will lessen your sentence."

"I maintain I'm not guilty, Stuart. I will speak with my lawyer first. Where will you be going now?"

"The pull of Luna is strong. She waxes and wanes in the shadow of the satellite. I think I will report back in Terra's system and maybe make some kind of bold career move."

He's talking in code. He's referring to the broadcasting satellite and his planned attack. River fought to keep his facial expression blank. "Are you up to that, being out of action for so long?"

"One never truly loses what one once knew. I think some great general said that. I'm still sharp enough. Sorry I can't bring you along for the ride, but I must do what needs doing."

"Of course, I understand. By the Centre's light I wish you the best of luck!"

"River, I know you're deeply religious, but you do know that this Centre business is just man replacing heaven with the next *unreachable* destination?"

River smiled genuinely at his friend.

"'Bye, River. Look after yourself."

CHAPTER TWENTY-FOUR

The junior ensign stood by the large transparisteel window that overlooked one of the quadrants making up the gargantuan Luna-One spaceport. It was the Human Earth Confederation's primary base of operation and the largest space installation mankind had ever constructed. It stretched many kilometres in each dimension, and required tens of thousands of souls to keep it running, let alone defend it.

Its size was a necessity, though. It had been designed to allow almost every capital ship in the Confed Navy to dock directly with the spaceport via one of the hundreds of docking columns. Smaller fighters landed directly into the superstructure via one of the many hangar bays. The central structure looked like a massive hourglass, two orbs standing vertically in alignment with the north and south poles of Earth, connected via a tube that looked thin but in actual fact was a kilometre in diameter.

The ensign had been based at Luna-One for almost a year now, having served his first year in Confed on Earth first in New Houston. In his year he had never seen this many ships. All the docking columns were occupied. Walkers and crawlers moved along the outer hulls of the ships inspecting the joints and seals. Some of the ships were having new designations painted on their hulls as new fleets were created and subdivided into task forces.

The capital ships were not the only ones being reorganised; even the fighters had been redistributed into new wings and flights.

The sight reminded him of the days back on Venus, where his family had been in the business of farming honey. They had often needed to pull out one of the many combs to check on the honey production. The scene before him was similar to the way the bees had reacted to the intrusion, the little fighters flying about akin to the drones, the capital ships the queens and the walkers the worker bees. It was an organised chaos such as he had never seen.

He was not the only one in dereliction of duty. He was surrounded by the other young ensigns from his academy. They were equally in awe.

He picked up a change in the rhythm out there. An order must have been issued. The walkers all hurried for hatches and quickly disappeared into the hulls of the ships they had been walking on.

One by one the capital ships began to separate from their docking columns, ponderously swinging their bows away from the structure, some banking down, others pulling up. Their large aft, dorsal and ventral thrusters flaring energy to push their bulk in the right direction and steer their masses safely away from the spaceport.

It was a choreographed dance. Like one of the many romantic ballets his sister had loved to watch. Most likely still loved to watch.

He was completely entranced.

Slowly, but steadily, the capital ships fell into a kind of a columned formation as they distanced themselves from Luna-One.

They were heading for the Galactic Highway, that wonderful discovery by the once great professor from RF601. Fighters still swarmed around them, each fighter part of a wing flying in a wedge formation, the Wing Commander at point, with the lesser ranks forming up beside and behind.

He was itching to be on board one of those cap-ships. He was one year too late. He lacked the experience to be on board a cap-ship heading out into combat. He had been held back. Confed command had only wanted experienced crew on board.

Finally the cap-ships broke formation, as they began to line up to fly into the GH one by one. The fighters disappeared very quickly. They would be redeployed the second the cap-ship popped out of accelerated-space into real-space. The whole manoeuvre had seemed to last only a few minutes, but he knew that in actual fact the journey from Luna-One to the GH had taken at least an hour.

The scientist who had invented the GH had said that objects of mega-masses could not be too close to the GH. Something to do with gravity wells. The young ensign didn't understand the concepts, he only needed to understand the rules and processes of using the GH and the strategic value to the HEC. His job one day would be to man one of the many gun turrets on one of the class 2 cap-ships, like his uncle.

The GH lit up in a bright white light, and the first cap-ship flew right into the light. The light intensified so strongly that the young man had to avert his eyes for fear of having his retina singed. When the light disappeared the cap-ship was gone.

They all disappeared in the same way.

The war with the Ganymede Society of Life had begun.

CHAPTER TWENTY-FIVE

Task Leader Benision stood at the narrow viewport of her bridge watching the inky depths of darkness. In the distance beyond her vision was the gateway that would be letting the humans from Earth enter their hallowed dominion. Her task was simple as far as the letter was concerned.

"*Stop the enemy at all costs*," it had read. So simple.

The reality of her task seemed insurmountable though.

Have the Seating understood what it is that will be required? she wondered, not for the first time. The odds were stacked against the Hessr. The humans, warlike and aggressive, possessed centuries of combat experience and technology designed for utter destruction. The Hessr, simple and peaceful in nature, possessed meagre defences that were designed to mainly scare off would-be pirates or marauders intent on pillaging the contents of one of their many gas harvesters.

In the distance a brief light flashed; brighter than the light of the sun. Moments later, again. It continued in a steady pattern.

"All hands to stations, HEC in system. Stations to the ready. Send the signal to all Formation Leaders," she commanded her Task Assistant, who hurried away to relay the simple instructions. In truth it was an unnecessary set of instructions, any Hessr worth her mass would realise what the flashing light signified and would know what to do simply by logic. Yet order required it, and so she was duty bound to issue the instructions.

She turned and walked deeper into the bridge and

seated herself on her command seat. The command ship was a graceful ship, with sweeping curves. Two encompassing arms reached out ahead of the command bridge like arms intent on an embrace. Thousands of automated energy cannons dotted the surface. Unlike the ships of the Confederation, Society ships had no manned turrets. The energy weapons obeyed the mind of a single person, namely the Vessel Leader. She was the Formation Leader, she would not be directing the ship itself, merely the efforts of the whole defensive. The Vessel Leader would not even steer, she would merely choose whether the ship should attack or retreat during combat, or would issue destination orders when in normal flight. During an attack, the Vessel Leader would choose the targets, rate of fire and when to fire. The automated cannons would fire in synchronicity, maximising the impact. During the defence, each energy cannon would fire independently at whatever vessel on the scanners showed up as a foe.

Blindly she keyed the communicator's activation. "Array all ships in a concave, three layered line. Vessels furthest out must delay any form of fire until the Confederation ships are well within the concave arch. Return fire only once fired upon. We must sue for peace in this. The Society will not be the first to fire."

In the distance the flashing continued at its regular pace; one could be forgiven for thinking it was simply a satellite or a ship with its landing lights pulsing. Her scanner to her left betrayed the unfortunate truth, however. The top half of the oval scanner readout showed multiple red crosses, multiplying with each flash of light in the distance.

The war was coming right onto their doorstep.

Formation Leader Benision looked over at the Vessel Leader, her subordinate but still her peer. "The Seating should have allowed us to destroy the gateway months ago, like we had suggested."

The Vessel Leader said nothing. Agreeing with the Formation Leader would be a career-limiting move. One of the Ears was always within eavesdropping range. Benision, however, did not expect to see her family again. She could not see the immediate engagement going the way of the Hessr.

She activated the communicator again. "Activate the drones. Keep them hidden in the magnetic shadow of Callisto. As soon as the Confederation fleet passes by Callisto, have the drones block their retreat and provide us with the hammer."

She hoped to use the ancient hammer and anvil battle strategy. Though she doubted the Society's comparably small fleet would provide much of an anvil, nor did she expect the drones to provide a substantial hammer.

"May the light of the Centre be with us all. Strength to the Society," she finished, before deactivating the communicator.

#

Admiral Bennett had slipped into his cabin during the GH trip. Not that it was a lengthy journey. It was simply that it unsettled him greatly, the sensation of travelling faster than the speed of light. He wasn't even entirely sure whether anyone else perceived the strange feeling of time while flashing along the strange highway.

He was convinced they were not really travelling forwards. He felt as if his entire existence was being torn apart only to be reassembled again moments later.

Everyone else he had spoken to about the feeling had looked at him with narrowed eyes, then chuckled nervously before telling him that he was simply letting fancy take him. But he had been up and down the GH enough times during the deployment stages with that professor. He was sure it was more like hopping from one ring to another than being accelerated and travelling in a straight line.

He had during one trip been focusing on the distant star Alpha Centauri when they had been on a journey from Uranus to Saturn along the Virgo-Pisces Highway. The starlight had seemed to bend in a strange arch, as if reality had briefly bent the star out of existence and then snapped it back. The star had whipped up along his field of vision, and then slashed back in the same arching line, only coming to rest a few degrees back in a different location. Travel in a forward direction did not do that to a stationary object. The professor had been strangely evasive with his answers.

Since that day, the Admiral had found it better to be lying in his cabin on his bunk and to read something soothing. His First Officer would signal him of their arrival in the destination system and he would then resume active control of his ship.

This time around, their destination considered, he hadn't retreated to a novel as entertainment. Instead he had been reading reports on the expected defensive capabilities of the Hessr. It would be a massacre if the reports were to be believed, and he did not doubt them.

The superiority of the HEC was obvious.

The communicator buzzed, he reached out and activated the communication stream.

"Yes?"

"Sir, we have arrived in system and are peeling off to port to await formation orders."

"Good, I will be on the bridge in a moment."

"Sir."

He ended the communication, stood and pulled on his admiral's jacket; then left his cabin and made his

183

way up to the bridge. It wasn't a long trip. Down the corridor a few paces and up an elevator. The bridge was quietly proceeding with the general execution of tasks required of basic manoeuvres. His First Officer was awaiting his arrival and walked up to greet him, clipboard in hand.

Bennett waved him to silence, while he seated himself in his seat and pushed up a status report. Only then did he allow the officer to talk.

"Sir, we are in system. Callisto is off to our starboard side heading towards us. Jupiter is directly in front of us. Ganymede is just off to our port side bow, heading away from us."

"Are we beyond the magnetosphere?"

"Yes, but the Society's defensive line is just within it."

"Naturally, they know it will weaken our particle shields. Are their defences as we expected?"

"No, sir, they are a little stronger."

"Do we count many enemy ships?"

"Just over a hundred."

"Cap-ships?"

"Twenty."

"To our forty. And then over sixty fighters?"

"Yes, sir, to our three hundred."

"This will be a slaughter! We won't even need to scramble our fighters."

"No, sir."

He seemed to want to say more. "Out with it, Bamford. What's troubling you?"

"Sir, these orders are crazy. I know it's not our place to question orders, but the top brass could've sent three cap-ships to deal with this. Why the whole fleet? Three caps, even two, would've been enough to frighten the void out of the system."

"Jim, I agree with you. I don't understand it either.

But we're not here to ask questions. I hope that Command doesn't issue any kind of order I will have a hard time following."

"What are you saying, sir?"

"I don't really know yet myself, Captain. Let's just say that I might choose to not follow any inhumane orders."

"You'd risk a court marshalling for mutiny?"

"Something tells me not taking part in a massacre with our numbers won't go unnoticed. But at least my conscience will be clean."

His First Officer nodded, seeming relieved that his commanding officer had taken away a difficult choice for him.

The communications officer looked over at them and shouted across the bridge. "Admiral, we are ordered to the port-side of the wedge. The command ship will be in the centre of the wedge. We are to protect her at all costs."

"The command ship doesn't need protection. Helmsman, take us into position, five by five, and stable please." The helmsman nodded and began punching in the flight commands. Through the front viewport Jupiter swung out of sight to the right, Ganymede panned into the centre of the view and Callisto disappeared. "I want us to be steady and cautious. This whole thing might seem like overkill and insanity to us, but there may be a surprise lurking for us after all."

CHAPTER TWENTY-SIX

The now familiar jolt and dimming light revealed the blue orb of Earth just ahead of them, with Luna just below creeping into the blue. Stuart banked the *Intangible* away from their home world and angled away from the moon and the headquarters of the Human Earth Confederation. Their objective was not to return to their duty posts but to the primary broadcasting satellite.

They had just been about to leave Olympus when Jack's cousin had offered her services. It turned out that she had, prior to starting her business renting out escorts all over the inner systems, been a fully trained member of the Venusian Guard. Stuart had not been hesitant to accept her assistance; it had resulted in a beaming Jack and a smirking Jennifer.

"Rakers incoming!" shouted Jack.

Stuart briefly looked over at the large scanner screen. It clearly showed the rakers inbound on an intercept course.

"They must've gotten line of sight. We're flying into a no-fly-zone. They must've been watching this space closely," continued Jack.

Stuart just grunted acknowledgement. His attention was completely focused on the broadcasting satellite just on the other side of the moon. He decided to fly a tight line; it would take him close to the moon, skimming just along the surface. He would have to avoid and dodge some of the taller buildings that had been constructed on the moon's surface. But it would stop the rakers from opening fire on him just because they could. They would have to be more careful to prevent collateral damage from a missed shot.

"Unidentified stealth ship. Identify yourself. You are in a no-fly-zone," the communicator crackled.

Jack looked over at him. Stuart didn't have time to chat. "Don't answer," he simply said.

"Unidentified stealth ship. Cut your engines. You are in a no-fly-zone," repeated the communicator.

"Get Jenn to get suits ready, when we're near the satellite we'll do a space jump. You fly, take over the controls."

"A space jump! Captain, that's madness."

"No time to argue, these rakers won't let us dock neatly. We have no choice. Now shut up, I need to concentrate."

The moon was looming larger and larger in their viewports. The *Intangible* was not the lightest and most manoeuvrable vessel ever made by the Confederation. With all its plates designed to deflect radio waves and other detection mechanisms there hadn't been much room to install manoeuvring jets. The rakers would be far more agile, and that would work against Stuart. Fortunately, Stuart had no other options. The rakers did. That meant Stuart had to make this happen. His life, Jack's and Jenn's lives and the future of mankind depended on it. Nothing was a better bargaining chip than taking away all of Stuart's options. Thankfully, Jack didn't argue and instead left the bridge to go and relay Stuart's orders.

"Unidentified stealth ship. You have five seconds to power down and prepare for boarding. We will not hesitate to shoot you down," came the last warning over the communicator. Stuart ignored it again. The moon's surface was just ahead. Stuart rotated the stealth plates. It would bring some additional manoeuvring jets into play and allow his scanners to detect targeting locks. The targeting lock indicator light flashed almost immediately.

"Great!" Stuart complained to the empty bridge.

The moon's surface dominated the entire viewport, the detail of the dusty surface in full prominence. He looked at the aft-view camera and saw the rakers closing rapidly. He focused his attention forward again and in the last possible moment flared his forward jets, yanked back on the flight stick. The *Intangible* slowed, pulled up and levelled out, the weak gravity of Luna doing enough to pull the ship towards an impact. Stuart blasted the ventral and aft launch jets, catapulting the *Intangible* forwards along the moon's surface, tightly hugging the cratered contours. A loud crash from outside the bridge followed by complaints signalled his flying causing his companions to lose their balance.

He checked his aft camera again, and saw green energy fire splay across the moon's surface, filling up the area that the *Intangible* had just been occupying. The rakers, however, did not need to pull a desperate move; they were more nimble and had time to adjust their course. No more warnings were sent by them. They now knew that he had no intention of allowing a boarding.

He was hurtling towards the first Luna settlement. It had many high rises poking out from a large crater. His moon geography was poor, but he guessed it must be the Tycho Crater. Instinctively, he jinked to the left and energy fire flashed past him, again missing him. He closed with the buildings and only just managed to manoeuvre in between two tall buildings, avoiding further attack. The gaps between the buildings were narrow. Too late, he noticed the risk of what he was doing.

It *was* the Tycho Crater. The first crater that the Lunan government had decided they would cover with a large dome. The lattice was being constructed on the far end so that the sub-surface tunnel system could be removed in favour of a biodome. From the corner of his eye, he noticed that the rakers had decided to take a high line and fly above the city. The rakers had no need to be daring. They could afford to fly high and intercept him when he popped out of the city.

He slowed down. He would take the attack to them and surprise them and then fly on while they were executing defensive moves. He angled his nose up, activated the dorsal and ventral turrets into pilot-controlled mode. They would swivel forward, firing only in one direction.

He was astounded that he did actually surprise the rakers. They were patrolling the far periphery and did not expect him to come blasting out from the top of the city. He released his own green energy fire towards them, hitting one of the rakers on its energy shields. The shields flickered and flashed with electrical energy then winked out. It would be some time before that raker would have protection against another energy attack. The other evaded his fire.

Both began to execute routine defensive flight patterns, but Stuart was not interested in shooting them down. Instead, he brought his nose down and pointed the *Intangible* at the broadcasting satellite. His scanner began to beep. More rakers were joining the fight, but they were some distance off. The same distance he was from the satellite. They were coming from Luna-One.

He reached for the announcement switch. "Jack, get up here, you must take over."

One eye on the scanner, another on the quickly approaching satellite, Stuart felt his hands get clammy with nervousness. The space jump was looming up.

Jack burst into the small bridge. "Yes, Cap?"

"Take over, watch for those fighters. Try and get us close so we don't need to be lucky with our jump. I need to suit up. I've angled all our energy shields to the back, we have five hundred centimetres of shield. We can take two or three full hits. That's it. I've dropped the particle shields so we can jump. I just hope they don't have mass drivers."

"Got it, Cap."

Jack settled himself into the co-pilot's seat.

"Good luck."

"Thanks, Jack."

#

The wedge formation was burning brightly on the scanner's readout, a sea of blue crosses moving steadily towards an arch of red squares. A digital readout desensitised the act of war to basic colours lacking any real emotion. The grey circle of Callisto shimmered off to the edge of the scanner's display. It seemed slightly fuzzy, but the Admiral realised that it was probably just his imagination. Monitors these days were so crisp that no image was ever vague or unclear, unless the broadcaster wanted it that way.

Jim Bamford, his First Officer, was standing a few steps ahead of him speaking with the Communications Officer. The bridge of the *Agamemnon* was large; it took a substantial number of personnel to coordinate all the activities necessary to operate the large capital ship. Though the *Agamemnon* was large, she was designed not for all-out attack but, rather, to pull ships out of sub-light speed into speeds that would make military activity simpler to execute. Her size contributed to that exercise. As the *Agamemnon* generated a substantial gravity well, navigation computers would confuse the gravity with that of a celestial body and would cut the sub-light engines to avoid a collision, sounding off the alarms and ejecting crew from their stasis.

It remained to be seen whether the *Agamemnon* still

had a place in the new order of the Galactic Highway. The Admiral had a hunch it would. The technology was still young and they had not had the opportunity to test the theory yet, nor any real limitations and risks.

Jim approached his command seat. "Admiral, we have received our orders. We have engaged the ships at the far end of the convex defensive line. And are beginning to pull the convex shape flat. Once we have achieved that we are to disengage and start up our gravity well and stop any ships from entering sub-light speeds," he relayed.

"They mean to end them this day. One single attack."

"It would seem so, Admiral."

Bennett thought his options through carefully.

"What are your orders?" asked Bamford. The whole bridge was looking at him with expectation in their eyes. The Admiral was fully aware that not one person on his bridge agreed with this offensive manoeuvre. His decision would earn him endless respect or eternal loathing. He was a man of honour, he believed, but also a man of duty.

"Our orders are to engage, they do not state that we must decimate our opponent. I am sure other capital ships have been similarly deployed. We shall proceed at patrol speeds, fire some shots. By that time, the defensive lines will have broken, and we can pull back. First Officer Bamford, if you please."

Jim nodded and strode off to see Bennett's orders carried out, his back straight with pride. The rest of the bridge looked relieved that they would not be called to a duty that was inhumane and tasteless. The Hessr may be guilty of attacks, but Bennett had a hard time believing that. He had dealt with one of their Chairs before. They were an enlightened people and seemingly at peace with their small place in the universe.

Bennett looked out of the starboard viewports at the other ships in the fleet; many much smaller than the *Agamemnon* but more heavily armoured and armed. The wedge was still keeping formation, though that would not last much longer. The command frigate was in the middle of the wedge. Bennett could make her out clearly. She was long and heavily armoured. The GH wasn't large enough to transport carriers or Dreadnoughts, fortunately for the Hessr. Frigates and destroyers were dangerous enough, however.

"Fighters incoming!" called one of the tactical officers from his quarter scanner.

"I want warning shots fired, no shots to kill. Our particle shields will withstand their fire for the first while," ordered Bennett, swinging his command chair around to be able see out of the aft starboard viewports. He could only just visually make out the GSOL fighters against the dark backdrop. Red energy fire flashed out, but cascaded in an electrical storm against the energy shields of the *Agamemnon.*

"Stat report, how much weaker are our shields?" called out Bamford.

"Not even two per cent, sir," answered the shields operator.

"Fire warning shots, make them close to not make it too obvious to the Fleet," ordered Bamford.

Various offensive officers spoke into the comm links to the gun command further in the bowels of the cap-ship; shortly afterward, green energy fire lanced out towards the fighters, missing them narrowly. The *Agamemnon* had some of the best gunners in the Confed Navy. She needed them, since she was so much poorer off with regards to raw firepower. Her gunners needed to be all the more accurate. The GSOL fighters began evasive manoeuvres.

"Be careful with the shots now, I don't want us

hitting them by accident," cautioned Bennett.

"Too late," sighed Bamford, as a green energy shot flew outward, obviously intent on missing the fighter. The fighter chose at the last minute to weave in an attempt at evasion, only his weave took him straight into the shot. The fighter erupted in a liquid ball of flame, consuming in on itself and winking out of existence.

"Survivors?" called Bamford out at one of the life form monitoring operators.

"None, sir."

"Damn it. Attack Officers, order your men to be more careful," Bamford shouted.

"Captain Bamford, please withdraw us. Have word sent to command, that we have succeeded in drawing out their defensive line and will move to our second task of starting up our gravity well. When we have reached our destination, scramble our fighters. I would like to engage any incoming GSOL ships at a safe distance from our turrets. Our pilots should be able to keep them in a stalemate for some time. Order our Wing Commanders to treat this as a dogfight exercise. I don't want any kill shots taken. If they can disable the fighters, then good."

#

Stuart rushed to the airlock, where Jenn was waiting for him with a suit in hand. She was suited up already, helmet at her feet, sidearm in a holster at her belt and a rifle slung securely across her back.

"A space-jump?" she questioned with a hint of amusement in her voice. "I haven't done one of these since basic training."

"Me neither, but don't tell Jack that," said Stuart while he pulled up the suit's trousers.

"Some rough flying there."

"Either that or us being sucked into the void." His answers were distracted as he busied himself with the jacket and the various seals for the oxygen generator.

"I didn't say I had a problem with the flying," she laughed.

"Help me with the back connections," he said, turning his back to her. She obliged.

"We're almost there, get ready to jump!" Jack's voice intoned over the announcement speakers.

Stuart opened the inner airlock door, pulled on his helmet and stepped into the airlock. He activated his radio.

"Jenn, I'm going to close the inner airlock, then hit the emergency release on the outer airlock door. The vacuum will give us an added launch with the decompression. You will have to use some of your stored oxygen to correct your flight. Be careful you don't over adjust. You could miss the satellite by quite a bit."

Her light-hearted demeanour vaporised. "Is there no easier way?" she asked nervously.

"Afraid not, you can sit this out, I can try this alone."

"No, I won't let you down. You won't get this right alone."

"OK."

"Guys! You've got twenty seconds," said Jack over the radio. Stuart closed the inner airlock, raised the protective glass covering over the emergency airlock release and put his hand over the push button.

"Ten... nine... eight... seven... six... five... four... three... two... one! Go! Go! Go!" shouted Jack.

Stuart slammed his hand down and the outer airlock door blasted away from the *Intangible*. The vacuum instantly ripped them free of the airlock. Stuart felt his whole body jolt with the force of the suction. He quickly recovered, his pilot's instincts kicking in. He released small bursts of oxygen from his suit. Spacesuits had a number of vents all over the back and chest that allowed for limited steering. It was part of all navy personnel's basic training to learn how to steer a space suit. It was a skill that was crucial to survival out in the dark depths of space.

He looked around in search of Jenn and found her far below him. She had also recovered and was jetting up towards the satellite in adjacency to his straight line flight. He looked over his shoulder and spotted Jack pulling away and heading back out of the no-fly-zone. The rakers had somehow miraculously missed their jettisoning and were pursuing Jack, ignoring them.

The flight to the satellite was short and the landing was hard. Jack had aligned them perfectly. *Thanks, Jack*, he thought in gratitude. Jenn hit a little lower down on the large satellite's hull. The service gantry was lower than they were, they would have to crawl along the hull. She looked up at him. He pointed down past her. She understood his gestures and began to move downward.

The gantry was a simple narrow walkway that ran the circumference of the satellite, so that technicians could get themselves to handholds easier and climb out towards various emitters or receivers. Stuart shimmied to the entrance hatch and keyed in one of the many key sequences he knew. None of the codes responded positively.

"We will have to blast it open, I don't see any other way in," said Stuart over his radio, risking interception.

"Is this an airlock?" asked Jenn.

"Must be."

"Honestly, I don't think that's the best idea. There must be an emergency communicator on the outside."

"Yes, you're right. It's a standard sequence on the keypad."

Stuart cut the radio signals, and pushed in the emergency code of five zeroes and a single five. The signal lights flashed alternately red and green. Within moments the airlock popped open, hissing with steam as the residual heated air escaped into the vacuum. They both fell into the airlock, and the hatch closed behind them. Through the small viewport Stuart could see three people trying to peer into the airlock. The airlock was refilling with breathable air. The inner door opened, Stuart wasted no time in attacking the first of the three people, knocking the first one out with a solid punch to the jaw. The second was surprised by the whole encounter, but the third seemed to be prepared. The man took a swing at Stuart and struck his stomach. The suit absorbed much of the punch but he still felt the pain lance through his abdomen. Jenn had jumped the second, wrapping her rifle barrel around the throat and was choking the man. Stuart, exchanging punches with his opponent, who seemed to have some brawling experience, was beginning to lose the encounter. A single shot fired over his shoulder felled the man. Jenn had dealt with her opponent and now had chosen to kill his.

Stuart ripped his helmet off. "Are you mad?" he shouted in a whisper.

"He was winning, we can't waste time," she snapped defensively. "Come, which way?"

"This way, I think." Stuart was angry; he had not intended killing anyone. It defeated the objective of the mission as far as he was concerned. *I will deal with that later, right now there is this mission and that's all.*

He recalled the layout of the broadcasting satellite from the documentation he had retrieved while on Olympus. It was a relatively simple layout. It had crew quarters on the lowest level, through a narrow tunnel that rose up to the upper levels that housed most of the broadcasting equipment. Most of the satellite was given to that function. It supposedly had only a single broadcasting computer.

"We must keep quiet, this satellite is manned by few individuals. We should be able to sneak to our destination," he whispered.

"You know, we never discussed how we will get off this thing safely?"

"We get captured, that simple. That's why I didn't want to kill anyone."

"Oh," was all she could say. Jenn now realised the error of killing.

#

The *Agamemnon* pulled up behind the wedge and turned to face the starboard broadside, towards the thickest part of the fighting, putting Callisto out of sight behind them with Ganymede hanging proudly just off the starboard bow. In the far distance the details of the battle were largely lost, occasionally an explosion would emit a variety of different lights and flames. Brilliant green and crimson energy fire played out from the cannons of the ships engaged in battle.

The energy weapons for the Hessr were fuelled by radium particles and these burned a crimson red, whereas the Confederacy used barium particle cannons that burned with a pale, apple green colour. It was an unintentional occurrence, but it struck Bennett as highly planned. Having different colour energy fire allowed the strategist to work out who was the dominant force.

The battle in the distance was predominantly green energy fire. The Confederacy, as expected, was winning.

"Admiral, sir," called an officer at one of the many scanning screens. "We detect a number of Hessr attempting to engage sub-light speeds."

"Is the gravity well holding them?" he asked, almost wishing that the reliable technology might fail for once. The admiral would have preferred it if the Hessr wishing to flee could accelerate up to sub-light speeds and get away from the much slower Confederacy capital ships.

"Yes, sir, the only corridor away from this sector at present is through where we are. All other directions would be too close to Jupiter and the sub-light navigation systems would not compute such a trajectory."

Sub-light speeds had for many years been the fastest way of travelling between the planets. The speeds were nowhere near that of light, though some vessels were capable of at least half the speed of light. The inertial dampening systems installed on all ships capable of these extreme speeds prevented the human body from being crushed, but sustained time outside of stasis chambers was dangerous to the body and prolonged exposure would result in heavy DNA-treatment and cell repair. The liquid-filled stasis chamber increased the dampening around the body firstly, but secondly also allowed for a deep hibernation sleep for travellers facing months or even years at sub-light speeds. It did occasionally happen that someone would need to travel to Venus from Uranus when those planets were on opposite sides of the sun.

At sub-light speeds a pilot had no control over the vessel, as the smallest adjustment to trajectory could result in a massive change in direction. Only computers were fast and precise enough to make the calculations and the adjustments to the flight path. If the computer calculated or detected a massive gravitational force bending the space–time fabric, it would not travel towards the well. In the event of a well being in close proximity, the computer would refuse to accelerate to sub-light speeds, forcing the pilot to stick to normal kph, or kilometre per hour, speeds.

Admiral Bennett stood up and walked over to the much larger scanning displays the tactical officers were perusing. His command console gave a rudimentary view and he craved more detail. The display revealed what he expected, but with a minor difference. The Confederacy was indeed winning the war, but the Society had exacted a toll. Far more capital ships than Bennett would have expected were now depicted as dark grey crosses.

"There are quite a few downed cap-ships?" he asked.

"Yes, sir, the Hessr work in synchronicity. They all attack one capital ship at a time. There is a flaw in their strategy, in that their single mindedness leaves them open to counterattack."

"I guess they figured they would lose anyways, and that they might as well take some of ours down with them," he finished off, feeling a sense of swelling respect. "What is that mass of white markers moving out from behind Callisto?"

"We haven't been able to identify those as yet. At first our scanners seemed to think it was simply a corona of static around Callisto, but as the battle has progressed the scanners have decided that these are objects."

As Bennett considered the objects milling around Callisto, Bamford joined them at the scanners.

"Sir, our shields are all at full and our weapons are primed. The fighters report that the Society fighters they had been engaging have pulled back and are joining the main fray. Should we recall them?"

"Yes, Captain, please recall them and have them hold a defensive perimeter around our position. What do you make of these supposedly neutral objects?"

Bamford looked at the screen for a moment. "Sir, this reminds me a bit of the history lesson. The one about the UER and the Guild Wars. The guilds had used mining drones as attack gunboats, but the UER's scanners had drones coded as neutral and never saw them coming."

"It's an attack! Bring all shields around and cover our rear. About turn, bring shields forward and bring those fighters back pronto!"

The bridge erupted into panic stations.

#

Stuart and Jennifer's progress through the broadcasting satellite was much slower than anticipated. The opening of the airlock via an emergency pin code had put the station on high alert and armed patrols were scouring the satellite looking for them. Undoubtedly, they would have found the body already. That discovery would have informed even the thickest of guards that the intruders were armed and dangerous. Their movements from chamber to chamber had been punctuated by cowering in dark recesses, too afraid to breathe, then short bursts of running to the next hide-hole.

Stuart was amazed that they hadn't been discovered yet. The guards at the station must have been of the lowest calibre and the most inexperienced. Twice he could have taken one out with an easily placed shot while hidden behind boxes that were stacked on a shelf, but the guards had each time simply looked into the room, and moved on.

To make matters more complicated they had no clue where they were going. Eventually, they stumbled into the broadcasting control room.

A man was seated at a console busy reviewing some briefing that was scrolling along the screen. When they entered, he turned and stared at them with a vacant and surprised expression. Stuart didn't wait for a reaction, he simply knocked him hard on the temple with the butt of his rifle, knocking him out.

"Bar the door," he whispered to Jennifer, who did as instructed. Sliding into the chair, Stuart started looking over the various controls. "Do you have any idea how this works?"

"No, but how hard can it be?" she asked over his shoulder.

"None of these buttons look anything like the home cinema stuff I've worked with."

"I guess it wouldn't," she agreed, sounding deep in thought. "I think I can see what needs doing, some of this terminology is familiar from my early days filming adult entertainment."

"Then have at it." He stood up and let her take a seat, placing the storage medium with the security recording on the control desk. Rather than watch her, he went and stood at the door with his ear pressed against the metal. He could hear the guards patrolling up and down the corridor. It seemingly never occurred to them that they should check into the control room, and that suited him just fine.

Only moments seemed to have passed when he heard the chair creak. Jennifer stretched herself, yawning. "That's it, it's uploaded and will air at the next ad-break on all channels across the solar system."

#

The exhilaration of battle took over and all thoughts of defensive lines or sparing the opposition got buried under an avalanche of self-preservation. Bennett took control of his bridge and began issuing orders that came as naturally to him as breathing.

The *Agamemnon* flew right into the thick of things, his defensive shields crackling as radium particle beam after beam rained against them.

"Switch to mass drivers, keep the shields strong, redirect all energy sources to the shields. I want nothing to get through."

The sounds of the mechanical mass drivers thrummed through the hull of the *Agamemnon* as the bullets fired through the energy shields. Energy shields were efficient at keeping energy fire out, but they also stopped retaliation. Old school mass drivers were needed in that event. They were not as effective as energy weapons, not being as fast and not having the same range. But when something was attacking you, you didn't need range.

"Admiral, we have an incoming Code 1 transmission, it's coming from our media room. Someone is requesting we view this," shouted the comms officer.

"I don't have time for video clips, Lieutenant."

"I think you should see this!" persisted the lieutenant.

"If this isn't related to the battle, you'll find yourself in the brig. Play it."

The screen at his command chair switched from a tactical display to a video feed. The face that greeted him took him by complete surprise.

"Good day, or evening, fellow members of Sol, whichever moon, planet or installation you are on. My name is Professor River Goldstein. Many of you might not know me, some of you might know me for what I

have been accused of, while others might know me for what I have contributed to life. Right now mankind is being manipulated by a sentient life form whose actual name is unknown to us but I have come to call it the Parasite.

"These Parasites are insidious, making their homes within our human bodies, tapping into our nervous systems, taking over our memories, our wills and our bodies. What they leave behind when they decide to move on is nothingness. Our souls are corrupted, darker than the depth of darkness.

"All human atrocities across the millennia can be traced back to these creatures.

"You won't want to believe me, but I have proof. Don't switch channels, I'm about to share with you that which I have seen personally. I have experienced the results. Once you have viewed this upcoming recording, I urge you to check those around you for scars just between their shoulder blades. Chances are that there are more people around you with scars than you care to recall. Expose these people to minor magnetic microwave bursts, and you will see the truth with your own eyes."

Bennett found himself looking up at a stunned Bamford. Bamford turned back to look up at the large video display showing a penitentiary cell with a man writhing on the floor, screaming in pain and agony as a wormlike creature was extracting itself from his back. Blood was oozing all over the floor. The Professor continued narrating.

"These Parasites are highly susceptible to magnetic radiation, which is why our neighbours from the Ganymede Society of Life have gone uninfected for so long. It is here, while the agents of the Parasites chased me from my own home, that I discovered the unequivocal truth. Right now, a war is being forged by

these Parasites. We don't understand their motives yet, but we have theories. I implore you all to evaluate the truths you see before you, and if I'm getting through to those of you fighting in the war around Ganymede, please stand down. The real enemy is not the Society of Life, it is…"

The video feed ended abruptly.

"Signal the retreat, cease fire and disengage. Initiate an open communication channel on the wide-band broadcasting wavelengths," commanded Bennett.

"Aye, sir," confirmed the communications officer.

"To all ships in the Jovian Sector, this is the HEC *Agamemnon*'s commanding officer Admiral Bennett speaking. All HEC vessels who feel this offensive is wrong are ordered to stand down and should join formation with the *Agamemnon*."

"Sir," shouted one of the tactical officers, "some of our ships are coming under friendly fire. What should we do?"

"Drop the gravity well!"

"Aye, sir. The well is down."

Bennett reactivated his communicator. "The gravity well is down, all ships under friendly fire are ordered to retreat back to Luna-One."

"Get the fighters back on board, and get us into sub-light."

CHAPTER TWENTY-SEVEN

Even though River had no view of the void outside of the enclosure in which he was sitting, nor of the flight controls, he could still feel the space–time fabric warp and bend as they jumped from one accelerator ring to the next. He was being transported to Earth on board a small prison ship; it was not a mass transport. It was designed for high-profile cases and accommodated only a few prisoners.

The kind of ship he was on was normally intended for the most dangerous types. He was being treated with greater caution than was necessary. Four other prisoners, who were a much rougher sort, accompanied him; many covered in tattoos, with scarred faces and shaved heads. His head had not yet been subjected to a shaving, although he feared he might get his turn soon. Not that he had much attachment to his hair, it was merely the last step in being a confirmed convict in his opinion.

The small room in which he was seated had six seats arranged in three rows, with him seated in the last row. Up ahead stood four guards each with an armed rifle; a small screen was mounted at an angle up on the ceiling showing inane video clips meant to entertain the prisoners. The guard got a message in his helmet earpiece; it was evident by the way he held his head.

The screen switched from showing entertainment to showing a newsreel. There was no volume, but the news reader was talking to a picture of River's face. Subtitle text scrolled along the bottom of the screen:

Less than four hours ago, the following video clip aired accompanied by the voice of, until now at-large, Professor River Goldstein. It shows a disturbing scene, which may not be for sensitive viewers.

His recording followed.

River couldn't help but smile. Stuart had successfully managed to get his video aired. It was a moment of success. He hoped it would spark what they had hoped it would.

The scene played out, and thereafter the guards looked at River with unusual expressions. The one that had received the message earlier pushed a security pin into the keypad at the door and slipped out.

"I guess nothing will change in my situation just because of a video," he sighed under his breath.

#

Even with the air regulators working away at full capacity, the heat inside the hydrogen harvesters was excruciatingly hot. Workmen wore only short briefs and shoes that had cooling fans built into the soles, the legs and torso bare and exposed; covered in a sheen of sweat. The harvesters always smelled strongly of body odour. Hydrogen was an important component in the production of electricity, and the best place to farm the quantities that were needed was in the close orbit of the sun.

Life near the sun, within the orbit of Mercury, was tough, hot and merciless.

Which is why his colleague's obsession with watching a frequent slice of the news was so frustrating to Blake. He'd rather have a movie to watch.

"Denholm, can we not watch something else? The news is just always full of depressing stuff," he complained, not for the first time.

"It's my half hour of information from back home," he answered calmly. Denholm was always calm, even when the sunshields were thinning and they needed to go out and repair them.

Denholm reached for the remote and upped the volume. "*Less than four hours ago, the following video clip aired accompanied by the voice of, until now at-large, Professor River Goldstein. It shows a disturbing scene which may not be for sensitive viewers.*"

The video clip that played afterward had them both checking for scars.

#

He'd been selling snacks and curios in the Olympian spaceport for many years, and never had he experienced such hype around a single criminal activity. Especially rape. The Venusians had a strange perception of rape, it must come from all the desensitisation that being surrounded by sexual activities invariably instilled. At least, that was his opinion. He worked his way around his counter onto the narrow shop floor of his little cubicle to fix up one of the candy bar trays, which had been disturbed by a child who had wanted one. His ageing bones disagreed with him as he bent forward.

A sudden milling around outside his shop drew his attention. Every passer-by was focused on the big display board. The board normally showed advert after advert, and occasionally would show important news feeds.

The Channel-V newsreader, a fiery redhead, much in favour with the Venusians, was busy reading out some piece of news. He turned his hearing aid on.

"*Six hours ago (Standard Inner Ring Time), the following video clip, accompanied by the voice of the recently apprehended Professor River Goldstein, was aired on all major Earth broadcasting channels. Professor Goldstein was apprehended on Venus during his attempt to flee the planet. It shows a disturbing scene which may not be for sensitive viewers."*

The scene that played out thereafter shook him to his core. He found himself looking at every visible back to see if he could see any strange scars.

#

One thing Tom could say that he got out of that youngster's visit was peace and quiet. Ever since that day, all the pesky spies and agents watching him had simply vanished. He was under no illusions that he was beyond the sights of their telescopes, but for now he had peace and quiet.

He had found himself so comfortable that he'd even taken a walk along one of the canals that he had enjoyed during his first years with his now deceased wife. It had brought back many bad memories and he'd scurried back into his sanctuary. Safe behind impregnable walls and eyes on all corners and crevices.

He seated himself back at his desk and was trolling through news articles on his never ending quest to reveal the truth behind these Parasites. He typed in his usual search string and the first hit was that youngster.

Now what has he gone and done? he thought to himself irritably.

The video clip he saw brought a massive smile to his otherwise dour demeanour.

#

His office's lights were dimmed low. When he found himself at the end of a long, busy day he most often preferred to have the lights low and a glass of Uranian whiskey in his hands. His feet were up and he was watching the broadcast from his former student for the third time.

"This will have some consequences," he declared to no one in particular.

The Saucer had been an eventful place during the last while. Ever since Goldstein had fallen out of favour with the Confederacy there had been a constant query for someone to come to the Saucer from some scientist or another wanting to unlock his research. So far none had been able to make head or tail of the work. He put his digital reader back into its dock, finished his last sip of whiskey and stood. He stretched, reached for his coat and began to leave his office feeling very tired all of a sudden.

He had just closed the door when he heard his communicator ring inside his office.

To hell with it, I'm off duty now, he thought grumpily, then hesitated and against his will went back into the office.

"Edison," he answered gruffly.

"We are compromised," said the cold voice on the other side of the channel.

"Indeed."

"The Elders are displeased, Cleaners are being dispatched."

"This will not be pleasant, is there no way to ride this out?"

"I don't see a way, but we have been ordered to save a handful of Feeders and Breeders."

"How is that proposed? I would imagine we are substantially exposed?"

"You are to execute Operation Scalpel."

"You have not answered my question."

"Correct, I haven't. You are to include yourself in the Operation."

"I see," said Edison, before the channel went dead. He felt nothing. *That's strange. I expected this day to come. I expected to feel something.*

He locked his office door and removed his coat before seating himself at his console again. Systematically he began wiping all his records, his years of research and his copies of various student files and documentation. Finally he poured himself a strong helping of his prized whiskey. He took his time, even though he was sure of the urgency of his orders. He would never be able to escape the impending purge. The history books of his people all spoke of these events. Sooner or later, they were always discovered. It was a testament to his race that they had survived this infiltration for the millennia they had. The human breed was easy to manipulate and gullible. It had been the human penchant for acceptance and laziness that had made it easy.

He finished his drink, left the bottle open and the glass on the desk. He opened his desk's bottom drawer, and felt for the hidden recess. In it he found the still concealed handgun; it was an ancient revolver that still fired small bullets using an ancient hammer design. He had chosen it for its brutality and the false impression any security officer would have of it. Most scanners would not even detect the weapon as dangerous. As it was, he had avoided every single compliancy security scan that had taken place each year he had been stationed on the research facility.

He unloaded the cylinder and checked the timing and the bore of the gun, then checked the cylinder advancement before reloading the bullets. He stood, donned his cloak again and left his office.

#

Luna-One bent itself into the vacant bit of the void just ahead of the *Agamemnon* as they came out of the final accelerator ring. After having flown along at sub-light speeds for a short while, the Admiral had reverted to cruising velocities and entered the GH with all of the ships that had followed his mutinous instructions.

Checking his command chair scanner display revealed that the formation of twenty ships was grouping up again. They flew in a simple circular formation, the *Agamemnon* in the middle, with five ships forming up around him, ten in the second ring and the remainder in the outer ring. Many of the ships had not followed his call of mutiny. Either those ships had stayed behind to see the orders of Command carried out, or they were pursuing him.

"Bamford!" he called out, and his First Officer came jogging over from the far side of the bridge where he had been overseeing the formation commands' execution.

"Sir?"

"If I were in command of the offensive, then I would be instructing at least thirty ships to chase us here. Depending on how things were faring in the battle."

"That many?"

"Yes, and if thirty are coming this way, I would imagine we're in for some rough engagements."

"True sir, but with us being this close to Luna One, would they pursue us?"

"We must assume that they feel we're about to attack the core."

"Yes, sir." Bamford seemed to be mulling over the words of his admiral. "Do you think we should signal peaceful intentions to the base?"

"I do. Have that done, and then have us proceed at cruising speeds to the station to await an answer. I want us playing this safely. Have none of the weapons activated, I don't want any of the FF beacons to transmit anything unnecessary."

"Understood, sir." With that Bamford turned to have the orders seen to.

Time will tell what the repercussions are of my actions. May I be judged fairly, he thought to himself.

The immense station began to slowly grow in the forward viewports, and all the while not another ship arrived in system. Nor did any answers get transmitted from the station. The formations jostled around a little. Some of the ships were drifting outwards, but the tactical officer seemed to be on it.

"Sir," called the communications officer. "Still no word from Luna-One. Do you perhaps think it may be due to our shields being up on full and the defensive formation we are flying in?"

"It's a risk, but I see the merit in your suggestion. Lower our shields to fifty per cent strength, instruct the other ships to do the same."

Bennett switched his command display to the shields' readout and watched them slowly weaken. It left him feeling exposed and vulnerable.

They were some distance out when the shields hit their half strength setting. Soon thereafter came the reply from Luna-One. It intoned throughout the bridge. "We see you *Agamemnon*, you are to dock on DC One Fifty Two. We will send docking instructions to all ships in your subordination."

Bennett breathed a sigh of relief. "Bamford, I will be in my cabin, call me if you need me. Proceed to the docking column," he said.

A heavy explosion sat him back down in his chair. He glanced over at his display and saw that the shields had dropped to fifteen per cent. "Stat report, what just hit us?" he called out urgently.

The bridge was in confusion. Men that had been walking around were pulling themselves back onto their feet, those that had remained seated were still at their controls.

"We were hit by a broadside from the outer ring!" shouted one of the defensive officers.

"Take evasive manoeuvres, bring the shields up to full, enable mass drivers, return fire on anyone trying to shoot at us, scramble the fighters!"

The view from the bridge out into the void revealed that most of the jostling had put the ships that were busy taking evasive manoeuvres in the middle of a vice grip. Every single ship in the outer ring was firing inwards using both mass drivers and energy weapons, meaning their shields were down. The enemy was not playing for keeps, they didn't care if they went down as well.

"Send a call for help out to Luna-One – we need support!" he called to anyone that was listening.

CHAPTER TWENTY-EIGHT

"Take us right up to Luna-One!" shouted Bennett as the *Agamemnon* rocked heavily from a direct hit against the hull from a heavy rocket bombardment by a Class-A attack frigate.

"We could drift into the station!" shouted the helmsman.

"I don't care, we need to cover a flank and the energy turrets of the station could assist." He hated explaining himself, but the helmsman's complaint had merit. "Bamford! Where is our fighter cover?"

"Green Wing is covering our port, aft flank. Red Wing is gone," replied his First Officer.

"Damage report?" he called to the defence officer.

"Shields are hovering between nothing and four per cent. Hull armaments are taking strain. Forty per cent of our turrets are offline. Fires are periodically breaking out in various sections. Twenty per cent of our innards are sealed due to ruptures."

"Can we sustain an override burst to sub-light?"

"No, sir."

"Bamford, have us roll to bring our good side to bear. Focus all fire at one cap-ship at a time. Target the attack frigates first."

"Sir!"

The battle lines were becoming more defined, and the Confederacy, as Bennett saw it, was only just holding. The *Agamemnon* was taking the greatest strain, he supposed, since he was the only Admiral and as such was being targeted. The divide could only be between these Parasites and the uninfected. Bennett was a man who believed in what his eyes could perceive and the video was too elaborate to be constructed. It was not infallible, but it certainly needed to be considered. Such an aggressive attack from other Confederate forces was too coincidental, aside from the fact that Luna-One had not fired at the *Agamemnon*.

"Barrage of Heavy Rockets incoming!" screamed the tactical officer.

"Flak and brace!" shouted the defensive officer into his ship-wide communicator. Bennett gripped his armrest hard, bracing himself. The rockets hit with a tremendous explosion. The *Agamemnon* seemed to groan under the stress. The flak shower must've not been enough to defend against the rockets.

"I want that frigate gone, damn it!" shouted Bennett. "Concentrate all weapons at it, barium and mass!"

The *Agamemnon* completed her barrel roll. Tracer-fire followed the much faster green-burn of the barium particle fire as the gunners converged on the attack frigate, pulverising through the remaining energy shields and raining against the heavy forward armour. The sleek shape of the frigate made it difficult to target, but the *Agamemnon* gunners were among the best in the fleet. Plates of armour burst as the hull was punctured and debris started pouring out into the vacuum. The frigate lost its forward momentum and started drifting. A victory cheer echoed through the bridge.

Bennett found himself breathing a sigh of relief.

"Engage full cruising speed. Get us near Luna-One. Call all fighters to cover our aft," he ordered. "Get me a full damage report and status of all other ships in the area."

"Sir, fighters from Luna-One are heading our way. The station has finally scrambled its defences," called the tactical officer.

"Finally, keep your eyes open for them attacking us. Right now I'm not taking any chances."

His small command screen began listing the status

reports for all the ships in the area. Too many of the ships were coming back with status 'unknown'; that was a bad sign. It meant that the ships had shifted their allegiances and as such were not broadcasting on the friendly frequency. Of the ships that were broadcasting their statuses back to the *Agamemnon*'s query, there were only a precious few that could be considered above sixty per cent capable. The *Agamemnon* was by far the worst off, total status only reporting at a little over thirty per cent.

Bennett switched over to the normal scanners. The high-speed flight towards Luna-One had drawn out the fighting with multiple destroyers and frigates in pursuit. Their disengagement from the clustered fighting had freed up some of the frigates that had sided with him; these in turn were in pursuit as well.

I suppose the fact that we drew some ships back with us is a good thing for the Hessr, he thought cynically.

"Two Dreadnoughts have just popped out of sub-light and are bearing straight for us," called one of the tactical officers.

Bennett could only sigh.

The Dreadnought was the pride of Confederacy capital ships. Sporting the heaviest of armour and covered in particle-cannon turrets, rocket tubes and mass-driver turrets, a Dreadnought could hold its own in the most unfavourable situations. Exactly why the Confederacy had ever built these behemoths in the first place was still a mystery to Bennett. There were no substantial forces pitted against the Confederacy that would require such extreme capabilities. Nevertheless, of the three in existence, the *Victory*, the *Excellence* and the *Flawless*, the last two were heading right for them. He was hopelessly outmatched and his only hope was to get within the defensive perimeter of the station, which had far more firepower than he did.

Luna-One was slowly growing visually in the forward viewports, but not quickly enough. His interdictor was quicker than the Dreadnoughts, but the frigates and destroyers were quicker than he was. They were closing quickly.

"Fighters incoming from ahead!" shouted the officer from the scanners.

Bennett held his breath in anticipation. The fighters would soon be in range to fire off particle torpedoes, capital ship killing technology. Unlike a heavy rocket, which ignored particle shields and employed old fashion heavy explosives to decimate hull and armour integrity, a particle torpedo was designed to eliminate energy shields to allow for the efficient use of particle cannons to do even greater damage to capital ship hulls. Particle torpedoes could also not be shot down by other weapons.

"Tac officer? Please notify me when the fighters enter torpedo lock range."

"Yes sir."

Bennett began counting down the seconds in his mind. *One... twenty-one... two... twenty-two... three... twenty-three... four... twenty-four... five... twenty-five... six... twenty-six.*"

"Fighters in torpedo range. Frigates in range. We're detecting heavy rocket lock."

The fighters came within visual range and opened a barrage of barium energy fire, it buzzed all around them but not hitting the *Agamemnon*.

"The fighters are siding with us and engaging the frigates!"

"Bring the rear turrets online and assist those fighters, have our remaining fighters join them, but keep our course going forward. I want as much distance put between us and those enemy cap-ships. Bamford?

217

How fare our comrades?"

The First Officer looked up from the comm-station. He looked tired. "Most are holding. The drawing out of the battle seemed to allow some to recuperate. We're beginning to win the upper hand."

"Good. Let's hold on for a little longer."

#

Benision watched the Confederacy ships accelerate into sub-light speeds and flash off towards the sun and out of her hallowed dominion. She breathed a sigh of relief.

"Have our drones close the remaining distance and form up into a triple high and triple deep defensive wall. I mean to finish off these last Confederacy ships. What is our general status?" she asked of the Task Leader.

"Formation Leader, we are in strong enough shape to hold the formation you request. It will come at a cost, we estimate at least two-thirds of our remaining ships will not survive."

"Have rescue ships at the ready to collect any ejected survivors from those ships that succumb."

"Yes, Formation Leader, by the Centre it will be done."

"I surmise then, that the human Goldstein has completed his objective and the Confederacy is now aware of the Parasites."

CHAPTER TWENTY-NINE

River could feel the change in the motion of the transport ship. It might have been imperceptible, but over the years River's primary study focus had been motion and so he knew a change in motion when it happened. They were landing.

His perceptions were rewarded shortly thereafter when the guards received an order via their earpieces and began to assemble the prisoners against the back wall. Strangely enough, though, River was excluded from the assembly. He was ushered, still handcuffed, out of the detention cabin and into the central passageway, which also had the boarding ramp. He peered down the passageway and noticed the cockpit where two pilots sat busy punching coordinate sequences into the navigation planning computer.

So they're not staying here long, I wonder what's happening.

He wasn't afforded the luxury of thinking it through, as he was nudged in the small of his back none too lightly and herded down the ramp and into bright sunlight.

Earth. The scent of ancient oxygen, the feel of the perfect human gravity, the wind, the brightness of the sun. There was no mistaking the human home world.

River squinted into the sunlight, his eyes paining with the sudden exposure to the brightness. Slowly his eyes were adjusting to the natural light. They'd landed in what seemed to be a private spaceport. There were no high traffic volumes and no massive terminal buildings - simply a round tarmac platform surrounded by a neatly manicured green lawn and a narrow pathway leading to a low glass building.

He was nudged towards the pathway, a little more gently this time. He stepped towards it, noticing a black pinstripe suited man standing halfway between the building and the platform. He walked confidently towards the man, not wanting to seem as confused as he felt.

"You may undo his bindings, please," said the man as they reached him.

River said nothing while one of his two accompanying guards undid his manacles, rather choosing to study the man for any kind of facial expression that might give his intentions away. After the experience with the attorney on Venus, River had become exceedingly suspicious of everyone.

"Come with me, Professor Goldstein," said the man when the bindings were removed. River raised an eyebrow and looked at the guards, still choosing to remain quiet. "Oh, you have been released into my custody and are, for all intents and purposes, free. Provided you don't do anything untoward."

The guards jogged back to the transport that had begun to fire up its take-off engines again, the shimmer of the repulsers disturbing the air underneath the transporter.

"You have me at a disadvantage, you know my name and who I am, but I have no idea who you are," said River, finally choosing to speak up.

"Indeed. My name is Charles Deepwinter. I am the newly appointed Human Earth Confederacy Minister of Defence."

"The newly appointed Minister of Defence?" River was baffled.

"Yes, the last one made a rather unfortunate case for war. She has stepped down now. Surely you didn't expect your video to go unnoticed? Otherwise why broadcast it?"

"Oh, I see."

"Please, Professor, let us go inside."

The transport had kicked up a fair amount of wind. The air was tugging at their clothes, whipping the lengthy hair of the minister around. River nodded and let the minister lead the way into the building.

The building was a simple structure with small rooms to the side of a main atrium that led either to storage rooms down one corridor or out back to the platform or elsewhere in the complex that this building formed part of. River assumed that they were some distance from the nearest city. There was no visible sign of a public building in the skyline above the building or in any of the peripheral distances. If they were near a city, its skyline would be clearly visible.

Charles led them towards a small meeting room that had a single four seater round table, a coffeemaker and a water dispenser.

Charles poured himself a cup of coffee. "Help yourself to whichever you'd prefer."

River went with just water and seated himself. Charles took a chair opposite him. River had a flashback to his first experience in a foreign room with someone who had made a career out of talking to people and manipulating emotions. He was under no illusion as to what a politician did.

"Your video has caused quite a stir," started Charles.

"That was its intention. We couldn't think of a better way of getting the message across," replied River.

"You certainly did choose the most visceral method available to you. You say 'we', whom did you collaborate with?"

"The Society of Life, and my friend, a captain in the Confederacy."

"The Society?"

"Yes, the Hessr were among the first to believe the conspiracy and they are the worst affected by the parasites' machinations."

"How so?"

"They are a peaceful people. The Parasites are generating a lot of focus on them. Even the war against them is being architected by them."

"You have no proof of that. Surely? The Confederacy's war against the Society is in response to their attacks on our worlds. Ceres the most recent."

"Minister, I have been amongst them. They possess no such guile and profess their innocence. I believe them, especially after having witnessed these Parasites twice in the flesh and after having dissected them. Through my investigations I have come to learn a few physiological facts about them. For example, I am quite sure that they possess the ability to tap into the minds and memories of their hosts and take over their actions and intentions."

"Your findings are in line with the theories."

"There are many supporters of these theories. Including former Confederacy officers of notable ranks."

"I assume you're referring to the Commodore? He's well known for his fervour."

"Yes, he is one of them."

"Nevertheless, your video has caused quite a bit of chaos. There are widespread persecutions happening in most cities, not much different from the Spanish Inquisition of the second millennium. People are being hunted for simply being different, with no real substance as to their being actual hosts to these Parasites."

"That wasn't my intention." River felt very guilty all of a sudden.

"Be that as it may, facts are facts. No good deed goes unpunished."

"I would like the opportunity to remedy the situation. I could go on another broadcast and define the way to find the Parasites?"

"That would certainly assist. What are the methods?"

River hesitated. He had an overwhelming feeling that he had been led directly to this point. "How will I be assured that once I part with this knowledge I won't simply be disposed of?"

"If that were my intention, then there would be a fundamental flaw already."

"And that would be?"

"You might have told others already, which you most certainly have. This friend of yours, and these Hessr. 'Disposing' of you, as you put it, would not serve us well."

"OK. Magnetic radiation."

"Radiation?"

"Yes, not nuclear radiation. Magnetic radiation. A small dose will be enough. The human body provides something of a shield against the radiation for the Parasites. But make the radiation burst strong enough and the Parasites begin an involuntary self-extraction from their host."

"That sounds simple enough, what's the catch?"

"The host does not survive the extraction, unfortunately."

"There's no other way?"

"I haven't had a chance to investigate that yet. I would assume it must be possible, but I am not sure as yet of the effects beyond the merely physical. If my suspicions are correct, and these Parasites do tap into the mind of their host, then it's not implausible that they would leave behind a husk of a body without thought or soul."

"If that is the truth, then the host is essentially already dead."

"Yes."

"This radiation. Is it dangerous to us?"

"No, the human body is about three hundred per cent more tolerant of magnetic radiation than the Parasites are. A strong enough dose is all that's needed and that is still substantially lower than what our bodies can tolerate."

"The Hessr, by all accounts, are tolerant of far greater than we humans?" asked Charles. The Minister of Defence did seem to know many of the answers that River was giving, almost as if there had been some kind of research done before and he was simply testing River's knowledge or confirming sets of other research results.

"Minister, has there been research into this before?"

The Minister went quiet for a bit. "Yes. A long time ago. Perhaps six hundred years ago. All the research came back as inconclusive, technology was the limiting factor. Everything got covered up."

"Oh." River didn't know how to answer.

"Is that why the Society is so peaceful?" asked the Minister with what sounded like hope in his voice.

"I don't understand your question, sir."

"The Hessr, you said, are more tolerant of magnetic radiation. They live near Jupiter. I am assuming that a parasite without a host cannot get that close to any potential hosts within the magnetosphere of Jupiter?"

"Yes, and as I understand it, even if they were to infect a Hessr, they would not last within their bodies long as the Hessr are not more insulated than we are, merely more tolerant. Their cells are adapted to magnetic radiation."

"I understand," nodded the minister.

224

The room went quiet for a while. The minister seemed to be considering a number of facts or newly answered questions. River left him to his musing, fetching himself a cup of coffee and slowly sipping at it. After having been in captivity for a while, he had been without coffee for some time and was enjoying the flavour.

"Sir?" River broke the silence.

"Yes?"

"We must expose as many Parasites as possible within the Ministry. There will undoubtedly be a number of them."

"Yes, I would assume so. We know something of their motivations. Learned nine hundred years ago."

"How so?"

"Nine hundred years ago, towards the end of the Guild Wars, a Parasite came to the UER ministers."

"What?" exclaimed River. "It turned itself over?"

"Yes, it went against everything their people stand for apparently. But the UER had come to suspect that an external influence was procreating the war between the mining guild and the UER. Due to this reason, supposedly an order had come about from some ranking source within the Parasite orders to purge themselves from involvement. The Parasite was sympathetic with the humans, and so wished to share some information. The host's body was eliminated during a move to a more secure facility and only a bit of information was passed on. The technology of the time limited our ability to discover more about them. The UER chose to cover it all up, and to eliminate all evidence. It was the wrong choice."

"I'd say. If they had not covered it up, we might have been spared many more years of turmoil and might have been more enlightened by now."

"I'm not sure about enlightenment. Coincidentally,

these Parasites are known as the paraci amongst each other. We know that they are highly hierarchical. We also know that they breed only when able to feed on the hormonal discharges that certain emotions generate, most prized being fear and terror. Additionally, we know that not all paraci are able to breed. We were going to discuss more, after he'd been moved, but that never happened."

"It stands to reason, then, that having paraci within command structures and decision making structures is critical to their breeding activities?" reasoned River.

"Precisely."

"Surely you can simply check everyone's backs?"

"Where? Within the Ministry?" laughed Charles.

"Well, yes." River was surprised by the Minister's sudden mirth.

"You have never been around a lot of politicians, have you? You can't just check on everyone, there are protocols, issues of privacy. The Ministry is flooded with process and procedure, red tape."

"What if we expose every minister to a burst of radiation?"

"We couldn't do that individually, news would spread and we'd at most be able to do that to one or two. But, we could do that at the next Annual Confederacy Council Meeting of Ministers. That is in a few weeks."

"I think that is too long," River argued.

"It will take time to arrange everything."

"Sir, the longer we take, the more likely it is that all this will blow over and the impact of my discoveries will be forgotten."

"Then I will call for a closed session regarding the war with the Society. It will prompt many to be present, if not most."

CHAPTER THIRTY

Charles had deposited River in a small, wood panelled side room of the main ministerial chambers. The main area was an amphitheatre shaped room with a small stage and pulpit in front of a tier of seats. The side room was comfortable, in a utilitarian kind of way. It had soft, brown leather couches and a plethora of heavy tapestries and carpets. The entire room was designed for insulation. Charles had called it the witness room. He could only guess what that meant. River was to be a subject matter witness for Charles' closed meeting. As a witness he would not be privy to the discussions of the ministry, but only used to provide expert analysis and information on the Parasites when called on. River, therefore, assumed that the highly insulated room was designed to muffle his noises from the ministry's amphitheatre, as well as muffle the voices and noises from the gathered ministers back into his witness room.

Charles had brought them from his estate in the grassy Greenland countryside into New London. The hop by transporter had been quite brief, mainly skimming over rough seas and to the tiny little island. New London was now located in the former Scottish Highlands. Since the seas had risen most of the British Isles had sunk, and now only a few dotted islands existed and New London sprawled across all of them. They had arrived very early, well before any of the other ministers. For preparation's sake the minister had desired their early arrival; supposedly there would be absolutely no chance of bumping into any other dignitary at the time they'd arrive.

After security clearances, surprisingly simple considering River's untried rape suspect status, they had been escorted to the ministry chamber. At first, River had been awed by the grandeur of the hall, but that had worn off relatively quickly. One hall could not compare to any of the incredible objects that the void offered.

The week prior to flying over had been used by River to gather various tech components so as to assemble multiple magnetic radiation emitters. These they had spent most of the morning installing in strategic locations around the chamber. The idea was simple: during the middle of the assembly River would irradiate the ministers for a few seconds and hopefully manage to expose a number of Parasites. Charles had initially been reticent to follow through with the plan, worried about the human right to life and feeling that this would, in essence, be snuffing out life. It had taken River some time to sufficiently explain and argue that once the paraci took hold in a host, it wiped all sentience.

Emitters installed, he'd found himself in the witness room. The assembly had started and he'd tried to overhear the proceedings by holding his ear against the door but had only heard muffled, unintelligible voices.

Against his will and from sheer boredom, River fell asleep. He'd been sleeping for only a few minutes when the door opened and a uniformed guard stepped into the witness room.

"Professor Goldstein? Please would you join the Ministry?" the guard requested.

River lifted himself up from the couch, slung his backpack over his shoulder, and rubbed his eyes. He felt groggy from his short sleep but stoically walked into the gathered assembly of ministers. With the hall filled up, the grandeur was more apparent. The structure must have had capacity for well over a thousand people. River realised that he had never asked how many ministers were in the Ministry. It wasn't inconceivable that to govern multiple planetary sectors, planets, moons and other facilities it would take a number of ministers. Former governments of Terran countries, prior to unification, had often had over fifty ministers in their parliaments at some stages of their histories. The combined numbers of all the countries prior to unification would in its own right total over a thousand.

He was led to a small booth to the side of the primary cluster in the centre of the small stage. He was seated and a microphone was set up for him. The guard briefly rifled through his backpack, even though it had been scanned during his arrival, then left to return to his post at the side of the assembly.

"Ladies and gentlemen of the Ministry, please let me introduce Professor Goldstein of the Research Facility 601 in orbit of Titan. The inventor of the Galactic Highway, and the individual behind the recent discovery of proof of these paraci existing," said Charles from his place on the stage, his voice amplified throughout the hall. A murmur arose amongst the ranks of ministers, undoubtedly many connecting him with the rape side of the story, rather than the video he had aired. "Welcome, Professor Goldstein. Thank you for taking the time to speak with us here today. We appreciate your knowledge on the subject of the paraci."

River, unsure of himself now that he'd been exposed to so many people, leaned forward and spoke into the microphone, "Thank you…" A piercing tone of feedback rang out forcing River to retreat a little from the microphone. "Thank you, Minister, it's my pleasure."

Charles continued without interruption. "Please, Professor, can you elaborate a little bit on your discovery regarding these paraci, as well as relate some of your personal experiences dealing with them."

"Certainly, Minister."

"We will at the end take a moment for some questions. Madam Chair, if I could please ask my fellow ministers to please show respect towards the Professor, who has been through fair amounts of personal ordeals in order to be here with us today?"

River hadn't noticed the woman seated further behind them, in an elevated position above the small stage. She quite obviously had been appointed to preside over the meetings, and to keep exuberant ministers within the borders of protocol. The woman said nothing, and just nodded her head in agreement to Charles' request.

"Please proceed, Professor," she said.

"Uhm." River hesitated again, collecting his thoughts. "I will assume that most here in attendance have seen the security camera footage that was streamed and also heard my accompanying commentary?"

"Yes, Professor, we have all seen the footage," answered Charles. "You may focus directly on your findings."

"All right, in the security footage that I broadcast, unfortunately the hosts died. The paraci during their urgent extraction tear themselves loose from the delicate central nervous system that is contained within the base of the skull. The severing from the cerebellum and the brainstem has the same effect as neck breakage. It results in either instantaneous death, or major paralysis."

The gathered ministers began talking loudly amongst themselves. The Chair banged a hammer, quietening the ministers down.

"Having two hosts and two Parasites to examine

gave me a unique opportunity. The first host had far greater soft tissue damage to the surrounding upper thoracic region, which is from the base of the neck to just below the shoulder blades. The second host had less soft tissue damage. This was due to this Parasite being smaller than the first, and in a larger host. Correlations or theories for the differing sizes of the Parasites are, as yet, unknown, nor have any theories been ventured.

"Closer inspection revealed that a tunnel had been carved from the thoracic region along the top of the spinal column between the T1 and C7 vertebrae where the Parasite makes its final home by hollowing out a cavity through the centre of the intervertebral disks that reaches from C7 up to C1, using its mouth mandible. It then attaches itself to the central nervous system and the brainstem using its many centipede-like legs, which are drilled through the vertebral body, the spinal process and the meninges into the white and grey matter."

"Sorry to stop you there, Professor," interrupted Charles. "Could you give us a simpler example? Perhaps with a visual explanation?"

"Yes, of course. Let me simply demonstrate."

River burrowed around in his backpack, placing various medical tuition models of the spine on the table. The Chair indicated that cameras focus on the model so that the large screens could show what River was indicating. River held one of the models up; it was a model of vertebrae with a side cut away to show the inner structure.

"If you look here and here, you'll see the intervertebral disc. Here is the section that is known as the nucleus pulposus, which is the centre of the disc. It's in here that the Parasite lives, and it burrows through here, the vertebral body, the spinal process and the meninges, and into the white matter, which is the core of the spinal column. The white and grey matter is responsible for transporting the electrical signals our bodies use.

"In essence, the Parasite sits safely surrounded by bone, and taps into the nervous system like a computer virus, catching all the electrical signals and in essence rewriting them. Making the host do as it wishes, say what it wishes and accessing all its memories and knowledge from the memory banks in the process."

Talking started up amongst the ministers again, as many seemed to begin to understand the implications of this and began cooking up their own theories. The volume began to grow and the Chair was forced to hammer for order again.

Charles spoke up in order to get the meeting to move forward. "Professor, could you please talk to us about how these Parasites nourish themselves?"

"Unfortunately, that is not something I have been able to discern as yet. Due to its location in the body, it would not be able to feed off what we normally would associate with sustenance yielding substances. We presume that the only form of intake available to it would be human hormones or other matter that is available in this spinal column. Certain substances are slow to regenerate, others don't regenerate in a single human lifetime. It is safe to presume that those are not food to this Parasite, otherwise the host bodies would have a short lifetime."

"Fellow ministers, at this point I would like to draw attention to the interview that took place nine hundred years ago with the United Earth Republic. It was covered up by our predecessors. I read from an extract; the complete document is available to each of you. 'Our people feed on the adrenocorticotropic hormone by extending our proboscis beyond the brainstem into the pituitary gland'. The hormone referenced here in the interview extract is the hormone that is crucial for regulating stress responses. Is this correct, Professor?"

"Yes, it most certainly is."

Again the assembled broke out in discussion, forcing yet another hammering session. The ministers understood fully the implications of what had been presented to them. The Chair continued with the hammering, causing the ministers to quieten down and listen.

"Professor, please could you elaborate on the witnessed phenomenon of these Parasites pulling themselves free of their hosts?"

"The conclusion we drew from our investigations links to an acute intolerance of magnetic interference. The human body is susceptible to this magnetic radiation, but not to the same extreme intolerances as the Parasites are. Our bodies provide a measure of protection for them – within our own magnetic fields, external influences are greatly minimised for them. However, in concentrated doses, it affects them as if they were not within a human host body. I estimate their tolerances to be about seventy-five per cent lower than ours."

"You were on Ganymede at the time of your event?"

"Yes, I was. In the extreme magnetic radiation that Jupiter exerts, even I was beginning to succumb to magnetic radiation poisoning. I had to receive DNA repair treatment."

"Fellow ministers and Madam Chair, I put it to you: with the ability of these Parasites to so efficiently disguise themselves from us, and considering the nourishment they need and crave, it is entirely possible that the theories that we have been purposefully covering up hold substantial merit. I further put it to you, that in order for these paraci to exist they must purposefully create situations that will provide for their people and in order to most effectively do this, they must work themselves into our power structures."

"Mister Minister of Defence, please make your statement and be careful of what it is you are about to propose," requested the Chair.

"Madam Chair, I put it to all that there may be a significant number of ministers present who are infected."

A loud gasp echoed throughout the hall. Many ministers stood up and began shouting in protest. Complete confusion broke out.

"Order! Order! The assembled will come to order!" The Chair was slamming her hammer repeatedly. Eventually she won out.

"Minister Deepwinter, you are making a very strong accusation, one with only the slightest glimmer of proof. How do you propose to address this?"

"As the Minister of Defence, I have the right to take immediate action if I believe the sanctity of our humanity is in danger. To address this threat, I have taken some executive actions that are well within my mandate. May I ask how many ministers are in attendance today?"

"Only three are absent. Less than half a per cent," answered the Chair. "Where are you going with this?"

"I have installed a magnetic defence mechanism. Let me demonstrate." Charles nodded his head and River activated the emitters with a push of a button on the remote he had taken out of his pocket.

Instantly at least a third of the ministers present dropped to the floor, writhing about and screaming. Ministers not affected stepped back, aghast at what was happening and shocked at what they were seeing. River assumed that they must also be experiencing shock that companions and partners had actually been infected without their knowing.

This will change the entire paradigm. Many will wonder just how deep this darkness has spread, he thought.

River released the magnetic emission. Nothing had perceptibly changed, the process of the Parasites extracting themselves continued unabated.

The Chair had come down from her desk, and came screaming towards River. River backed away worriedly. Charles came running towards them.

"Turn it off, stop it!" she screamed at him.

"I've stopped already," River shouted defensively.

"Madam Chair, this is part of the process. The purge. Look how many are unaffected."

"This is inhumane!" she retaliated. "Arrest them!" she shouted at the security guards.

Charles held up his hand, forestalling them. The guards effectively reported to him, not the Chairperson of the Ministry.

"The Parasites are inhumane, this is a threat to humanity, and this is within the realm of my mandate."

The screaming stopped abruptly. The hall was bathed in complete silence. Charles went back up to the address pulpit, and calmly continued on.

"You have just witnessed first hand that these paraci can exist in anyone, without us ever knowing. I move for us to declare a high state of Confederacy-wide alert." Looking up at the reseated Chair, Charles continued, "Madam Chair, please may I ask for a vote for the following: should a mass eradication purge be initiated regardless of the possible cost of human life, or should it be delayed in favour of discovering a detection process with a removal process that does not jeopardise human life?"

The Chair nodded. "Professor Goldstein, thank you

for your time today. You are excused now. The Ministry will continue to discuss the matter at hand behind closed doors."

River was led from the hall. As he passed by Charles he got a nod of thanks from the minister.

CHAPTER THIRTY-ONE

The orders were simple: get into the apartment and find out what was happening. He hated to be rough and tough, that's why he'd asked to be deployed on a research facility. The odds of violence on a research facility were minimal and in the beginning it had even been that way. Most people on board had thought him to be just a very bad engineer. But it seemed his thoughts had been completely off; RF601 had been prone to much activity and he had been busy almost constantly, disrupting one disturbance after the next. Even after that, the troublesome Goldstein had left the station in disgrace. False disgrace for sure, but still he had left under a cloud.

Jason stood in front of the apartment door, checked his watch and signalled the other guards at his back to get ready. He punched the override command into the security pad on the doorframe, and rushed into the apartment the second the door was open wide enough for him to fit through. Jason froze in his tracks. Of the guards that rushed in with him, only one managed to stay in the room, the other left as fast as he'd entered.

Blood had pooled in two puddles, some of it had begun congealing. Two bodies were present; one was Shiori. Her body had fallen forwards, collapsing at what seemed to be the knees and then pitching forwards face first. The other was Edison. His body was seated in a chair, his hand still gripped an old handgun, the back of his head was shattered and bits of brain mixed with blood had splattered against the wall.

Jason felt ill and queasy, his vision was swimming. The weapon that Edison had chosen was a messy weapon, energy weapons were far less gruesome. A single charring to the impact area, and the rest was internally biological in a way that Jason didn't understand and didn't need to understand. This was horrific. A tearing and rending of flesh in an explosive way. Like the mass drivers that fighters and capital ships used to tear away armour plating.

"You can wait outside if you like," he said to his one remaining partner. The man looked grateful, and quickly slipped out.

"Hello?" Jason said into his hands-free communicator.

"Yes, what have you found?" said the voice on the other side. Security command had requested the apartment intervention at the instruction of HEC command back on Earth.

"The Professor is dead, as is Doctor Wu. Looks like the Professor used an ancient weapon to shoot her and then himself."

"What kind of weapon is it?"

"It's a handgun – looks like a revolver."

"How did he get that on board? Why was that never picked up during the security scans?"

"Dunno, sir."

"Hmm, OK, check his back."

"Yes sir."

Jason went up to Edison's body, and spun the chair around so that the body faced the desk. Using his security baton he pushed the body forward until it slumped head first against the desk. Gingerly he pulled the shirt collar back with his fingertips and peeked down the back of the shirt. Protruding and hanging out of the back was a small worm-like appendage that was covered in torn flesh and dried blood. He felt bile rising in his throat and tried to swallow it down. He couldn't hold it and ended up throwing up on the floor beside the chair.

He wiped his mouth on his shirtsleeve, before connecting with Sec-command again. "Sir, there is a strange worm-like growth hanging from his back."

"Confirmed. Dispose of the bodies in the incinerator."

#

After the proceedings at the Ministry meeting, River and Charles had flown back to the Greenland estate. River had anxiously requested that Stuart be located, and his wish had been granted. Messages had been dispatched once River had explained the last known whereabouts of his friend. It wasn't inconceivable that Stuart had been taken into custody. In the context of things, River was confident that Stuart would be released from any form of custody with relative ease.

It was, however, clear to River that although he wasn't in any kind of imprisonment, he was still in a form of detention. Charles had kept him close and included him in all the proceedings as they occurred. From the minister's estate they followed the purge as it happened. Ironically, most of the paraci were seemingly killing themselves off.

His scientific opinion had been asked for on numerous occasions and he had been informed of what seemed to be various sub-breeds or races of the paraci coming to light. There were green, black and red colour variants. Not in brilliant colours, but there was a definite shade difference between the various paraci.

The Hessr had for the first time in hundreds of years come back to Earth and were assisting the humans with the purge, at their suggestion. Due to their genetic protection against radiation, they could be involved in purging operations for longer than a human could be. It was also in their best interest to be involved; peaceful humans meant peaceful lives for themselves.

River was seated in what had once been the dining room. The large table had been annexed by screens and computer systems with numerous people walking in and out of the room. River had been joined by anthropologists, theologists, sociologists and biologists. Practically the entire scientific world was abuzz. This was only the second entirely different life form to be discovered in the universe. The first had been the Bloon living in the system of Gliese. Few had travelled there due to the fourteen years it took for the fastest sub-light ships. Whole families needed to complete the trips and the Confederacy had retrofitted frigates for that purpose. The GH would change that journey into mere days.

"We've found more suicides among the paraci," said Charles as he entered the room. He handed the little folder over to the anthropologist, who jumped up at the mention of suicide.

River had kept his distance from the people after having been introduced. He had a sense of overprotectiveness regarding the paraci, almost as if he considered them his territory.

"It seems to me like they are executing themselves as part of a big cleanse," said the man while he flipped through the folder.

"Matching our purge?" asked Charles, but the anthropologist didn't answer, preferring to dig through a stack of papers. Charles ignored him and looked at River. River sensed the minister had something important to discuss with him. The minister left the dining room and River followed him out into the passage.

"Professor, you have been given a rare opportunity and I would most welcome it if you accepted," said the minister.

"What is the opportunity?"

"The Ministry would like for you to replace your former superior, and for you take charge over RF601."

"That's quite a bit of responsibility you're placing on me." River was not entirely sure he wanted to be leading people. "What will become of Professor Edison?"

"Professor Edison was found dead, by his own hand in your accuser's apartment. She was also dead. As you'd suspected, both had paraci infections."

River wasn't sure whether he should rejoice or feel saddened by the news. He'd known and worked with the two of them for many years. With Shiori he knew that she had only recently been infected, with Edison it was any man's guess. River settled on the thought that Edison had been infected for a number of years; it at least explained the man's terrible nature and his dislike of him.

"What's prompting this offer?" he asked of Charles.

"You are credited with two major discoveries, the Galactic Highway and the paraci. The Confederacy is unanimous in the offer of granting you a full facility to work on more discoveries. You'd have substantial resources available to you and a substantial pay-rise."

"Any requests for research?" River had a feeling the offer came with a catch of some sort.

"Well, now that you ask." The minister was smiling broadly. River laughed. "We would like you to dedicate substantial efforts in further analysing the paraci, especially with the discovery of other breeds or races. If there are physiological differences to the breeds, et cetera."

"Can do. The Saucer had few biologists, I'd need some more of those."

"Done."

"Anything else you'd want me to work on?"

"The GH. Some of us are wondering if there is a way to increase the distances between rings or perhaps even make it more mobile. In other words, so that individual ships are capable of achieving those speeds independently of the rings."

River considered the request for a bit, humming to himself as he did. The minister waited patiently for a response.

"There would be some substantial experimentation needed. In the simplest terms, yes, these requests may be possible. Resources, energy required, viable energy sources and risk to life, et cetera all come into play."

"Is that a yes?"

"Yes, it is."

"Great." The minister held his hand out to River, who took it and shook it readily.

CHAPTER THIRTY-TWO

"A new year, and a new order. The office suits you, River," said Stuart as he walked into River's new office.

River greeted him warmly, coming around the large desk that for now was still neat, having no mountains of paperwork stacked all over it. "Man, it's good to see you, Stuart. I got rushed off Earth so quickly and back here that I had begun to think that Confed wanted to keep me from speaking with you."

Stuart just laughed. "Quite the office you have here."

"Oh, it's nothing."

"You inherit this?"

"Hell no. Edison's office was further inside the Saucer and had no windows out."

Stuart and River both walked to the massive window that dominated the view out. Titan was hanging just below the Saucer and out in the distance was the orb of Saturn surrounded by its rings. They were on the dark side of Saturn at the moment, and that simply made the other five big moons look like bright lights hovering on a plane in line with the rings.

"The view is like I remember it from three years ago."

"Has it been that long?" asked River, having completely lost track of time.

"You think it's all over?"

"No, the solar system is beyond big, our galaxy even bigger. As it stands, to get to our nearest known neighbour with life, Gliese, takes us fourteen years. The Centre alone knows where the paraci come from."

"You got any ideas?"

River had to laugh. "No, Stuey, I don't. I wouldn't even know where to start looking."

"Have you started working on any of those requests?"

"No, I've been here for two months and most of it has been bureaucracy, moving offices around, setting up schedules, reviewing work assignments, ordering stock, retrofitting labs, the list is endless."

"Oh," shrugged Stuart.

"What of you? What's next for you?"

"I'm being assigned to you; well, kinda."

"What do you mean?"

"I'll be on that." Stuart pointed out of the window at a Dreadnought that floated into view from above the station.

"What, as an admiral?"

"By the void, no, only as First Officer."

"Only as First Officer, that's a big jump."

"I was Captain before. I've just been promoted to Major now, that's all."

"How is this linked to me?"

"Only indirectly. We're supposed to be the first to test anything you deliver, otherwise we have outer sector patrol together with the *Flawless*. The *Victory* has the core sectors. Our orders are to hold near your location, the *Flawless* will always get the other side of the sun to our location. So we won't ever be static."

"Oh, makes sense, I guess," River said. Military tactics still escaped him.

"So what now?"

"Who knows, Stuart? None of us will truly ever know the real depth of this darkness. I am left wondering whether perhaps most of the darkness we're blaming on the paraci didn't come from within ourselves. I think the depth of darkness is greater in us humans than it is in space. Sometimes I think we're the real anti-matter in this galaxy."